The Desert Store Series

Book # 3

The Three Cactus Limbo

Bud's Garage and the Quest of the
Three Magi

By Patsy Stanley

ISBN 978-1-7369460-4-6

Library of Congress Control Number

2019919899

More books by Patsy Stanley:

Novels:
Addition Jones
An Older Wine
Emerald Hawks Flight
Avalon Blue's Quest

Illustrated books for all age readers:
Christmas Stories From the Crone's Castle
The Dreadful Noises of Landoshar

Native American:
Red Leaf
The Green Mountain Shaman

Metaphysical book Series:
The Mental Body
The Spiritual Nature of Atomic Structure
Sound Energies
Shield Energies
Chakras, Meridians, and the Color Energies
The Elements

The Desert Store Series:
Book One:
Cowboy Johnson's Desert Oasis
Mama and the '57 Mercury

Book Two:
The Red Cactus Desert
Geena and the '59 Dodge Lancer

Book Three:
The Three Cactus Limbo
Bud's Garage and the Quest of the Three Magi

Book Four:
Susan Sugar Diamond
Away in a Desert

Table of Contents

Hello from Ben, Andy, and me.

The following is a short list of sayings that mean the most to us three gents:

Ancient legends are valuable sources of lost knowledge.

Take actions without words.

Tame your attitude.

The silence between friends speaks best.

Where words fail, snow still speaks.

Here is Miss Emma's short list:

Words contain the exquisite nightmares of the Shadow.

Hearts with words speak with care.

Hope is the thing with feathers that perches in the soul and sings the tunes without the words and never stops at all.

Emily Dickinson

Kind words cling and sing to the hearer's heart.

We work to find ways to say things we have no words for.

Distance cannot be cured without closeness.

There is more power in one simple action than in a mile long string of words.

Something wise from William the Dude

Ummpff.

Eskimos have fifty two names for snow because it is so important to them. There ought to be as many names for love. M.A.

Chapter One

There was a first love, but never a second for the three of us....

I was born full of fear that neither I nor anyone else I ever met could understand. It seemed as though I didn't have the veil over my eyes other people did. I was a soul without enough covering. Everybody else seemed to have at least a patchwork quilt to hover under, maybe a slick, thick hide. I didn't have either one. I understood too much of what it meant to be here on Earth, and it kept me terrified. Whatever the undertaking was I went through to get here, I did not know, but I did know this was a hell of a place to visit. Visit, because I knew I wouldn't get to stay. Nobody did. It was birth and death and whatever you got in between. A huge, raw place, beautiful and unpredictable, full of pain and pleasure. The likes of which has stayed huge to me all of my life.

When I was young, I kept trying to find others who were in the same trouble I was in, rowing the same boat, who knew what I knew, but there wasn't any around. I never found anyone whose soul was as astounded at showing up here as strongly as mine was. Mine was a lone soul in torment, without any way to explain my misery to the general public I shared this world with. If there were others out there like me, I never found them. My guess was they probably turned to religion and maybe found some comfort in it. I didn't see how they could, but what the hell did I know about anything? After awhile, I stopped searching, for people gave me odd looks anyway, so I shut up and hid.

Yep. It's true. I showed up this way. I was born into a small world in a small town. If a person acts weird in a small town, somebody will take them out one way or another. By breaking them. By making them become like they are. Or killing them off some way, or having them toted off to Fairview, the local mental hospital, or sending them off on the ten P.M. Greyhound bus to "visit" far away relatives.

I learned quick that being different in a small town is a dangerous thing. There is no doubt whatsoever that sooner or later, someone will try to take you over and try to convince you to use your life in service of their ideas. And it ain't just the Mayor that does that stuff, either. How far they take their convincing of you depends on your guts, the town, and a few other things. My small town was old and rigid, filled with old meanness and old secrets. The Shadows loomed large above Ardenville. The dictionary says that a small town is a human settlement larger than a village and smaller than a city. Ardenville fit right in there.

I write books. Small ones. Manuals. About how to fix cars. They chose me out of six men because they liked my last name the best. Spinner. Bud Spinner. Better being called Bud than being called junior, after my father. Nobody around here knows I write car manuals. The money from the books goes into a bank over in Stoverton, another small town about a hundred miles away from here. A town where nobody knows me. Works better that way.

Each morning I wake up alone with this awful flat feeling inside. No excitement. I don't want to die or live. It's not that kind of feeling. It's not being scared of dying. It's of having to go through some more of life without anybody. And not knowing whether having somebody would make any difference anyway.

Maybe it's depression of some kind. I always wake up in the mornings like that. Have ever since I can remember. It got worse after I turned ten. That's when I realized that someday I would have no choice except to die. Everybody else did, and I would have to take my turn, just like they were forced to.

There was nobody around to give me answers to the questions I couldn't ask. I couldn't turn to a church for answers, for we didn't go. Don't get me wrong. I have always been glad for that part. Religion was a waste of time to me. Always has been. It just wasn't big enough to hold my worries.

Ten. That was the year my mother ran away. She didn't leave with anybody. I was an only child and I turned out solemn and mean, like my father. At that time, I planned to stay that way the rest of my life.

Mother left on the Greyhound bus while my father was at work. He traced her to Philadelphia and went there. He came back and wouldn't tell me anything that happened, but he never spoke her name again.

"Don't you ever speak her name in this house again," he ordered me, not explaining anything. I didn't ask who, I didn't need to. I already knew. I stared at him. He glared back at me.

"And you needn't try to take off and find her. She don't like you neither."

That was the root of the damnation tree I live under. Not being liked. Or give a damn about. That kind of lonesomeness has been a faithful, bitter companion all my life. Just it and me. Until I became a roadie, that is, in my later years. An unexpected event that gave me friends for the first time and saved my life.

I never needed a babysitter back in those days. I stayed alone most of the time in our big, white Victorian house standing on the corner of Green Street and Main Street, where everybody passed by. There were four bedrooms upstairs and a big attic above them. Downstairs was filled with big rooms and big windows. Heavily draped windows and dark, large, heavy furniture. A dining room, pantry, living room, parlor, big kitchen, laundry and mud room made up the rest of the downstairs. In the small basement stood the furnace and hot water heater. That was about it for down there.

The front and back doors opened out on to a wraparound, wide wood porch painted white with green gingerbread trim. It looked like a good, big, noisy family lived in our house. A long, wide, concrete sidewalk out front led to the street, dividing the grass to be mowed on each side past the front porch steps. The big backyard held red roses and a vegetable garden when my mother lived here. It could have been a beautiful place to live in if the people living in it could have been different. That's why I never much gave a damn about the surface part of things, beautiful or not. Except cars. They are mobile, and that's what matters to me.

I mowed the front and back lawns and set the tin garbage can out to the street so Joe Smith could pick it up and take it to the dump and empty it each week. He took the can away, however full it was, brought it back empty, and set it carefully in its place against the corner of the house in the backyard under the big elm trees shade.

Joe was an old man who lived on the other side of the railroad tracks running through town. He drove an old truck, and it give him trouble all the time. Cars and trucks were easy to work on back then. They had carburetors, whitewall tires, and so forth. The car industry wasn't that old when I was born.

By the time I was seven or eight, I was interested in cars. I admired cars, not people. I was quiet and never said anything much to anybody. I disliked school and didn't want to "play" with other kids.

Taciturn and critical of others, I sat at the supper table each night and ate without a word if I could get by with it. Mother was a good cook, and the silence went on, and the dishes clinked, and the smell of the good food drifted warm around us. Sometimes mother got mad and tried to talk to us and managed to pull a few words out of me or my father. Then she gave up. I listened to the clock ticking in the hall. I listened to the sound of my mother ironing and running the wringer washing machine. I knew exactly where the floorboards squeaked and what kind of noise the wind made when it passed around the corner in the black nights of winter. Sounds came in the house from outside once in awhile. Other kids shouting, or a car backfiring. That was about it.

As far as I know, nobody ever got into our lives and learned who we were. I thought that was the way it was supposed to be. Nobody liking you, especially your mother, and you feeling hurt and put upon because of it, holding it inside, not talking. I got so I couldn't say anything. Not a word. I wished I'd known better. I would have spoke more to mother. I know to say that now, when it's too late.

Anyways, Joe's old truck was giving him trouble one Saturday morning when the dust lay still and deep over the parlor. It was the day my father ordered me to dust it for the first time since mother left three years ago.

The unused rooms never got touched after mother ran way. I closed the doors after she left, but father opened them again without saying a word. I would not go against him. The doors stayed open, and dust lay thick on everything.

I didn't want to dust the parlor, and father left for work, so I was outside fooling around with the lawn mower when Joe drove by in his old truck. The truck's engine was clanging like the decrepit fire truck old Jesse Owens drove when anything in Ardenville caught fire.

Joe stopped his truck in front of our house and got out. I watched him lift the hood and pull up the metal rod to prop it open. He leaned over and peered under the hood of the rusty, faded red truck. I edged over by him slow like, and he made room for me without a word. I looked under the hood and a thrill ran through me.

Now, I was one that was used to daily bad thrills of fear, little ones that run through me all the time. I was afraid of standing in that damn void. I stayed overexcited by fear on a permanent basis. No one knew anything about that stuff back then, and they don't know much more now. Besides, I let on like I had no troubles. It was hard, but I had practice.

I stared at that old engine and all the stuff under that hood, and my mind focused on it. I forgot all about my constant fear. I watched my hand reach under the hood and tunk real easy on a black hose and caress the top of the rusty carburetor. I turned to Joe and eased the wrench out his hand and turned back to the engine. Like me, it needed to run better. To not hurt. To have relief from some of the pressure. I waited until Joe understood that he needed to instruct me.

After that morning, Joe stopped by and we worked on his truck and he taught me. He was my teacher, and I respected him. My father didn't like Joe stopping by, but I had a hardened, troubled soul to deal with, and I needed Joe. So screw father. He got the message from my scowls and left us alone.

I never did give a damn about anybody's color or their religion, or political leanings, or whether they were ugly, mean, bad or good. All I cared about was whether they accepted me or not. And I could always tell which one was going on. I guess it was hard for anyone to dig deep enough to find me; to like me. People think they got to know you first. And nobody knew me. I was a stranger to myself too. One it was hard to get to know. I didn't know all my quirks, never have. I didn't understand myself and still don't know much more about it.

I did know that I was going to have a hard life, and it wasn't going to get any better, for I didn't have it in me to make it better and I better figure something out pretty quick. I was always in a hurry to figure something out quick back then, but nothing ever came to me, except to roost in Ardenville. I thought I had to.

So Joe taught me about cars. He talked, and I listened. He liked to talk. He said there would be cars made someday that would be way beyond our imagination. He said there were already cars way beyond his old Ford truck. He'd seen some of them over at the Dodge Dealer in Maryville.

Joe asked me if I wanted to ride over to the Dodge dealer with him next time he went. I wanted to real bad but couldn't bring myself to ride in a vehicle cooped up with another person that long. What were you supposed to say or do?

My father ended up dusting the parlor himself. I came home one day to find all of the rooms dusted again and a cleaning lady working in the kitchen. I'm dumb. At first, I just thought father wanted to freshen up the house. Then I grew a faint hope that he was getting interested in somebody besides mother, but he wasn't. I thought that if father could change, maybe I could too. I never saw any reason to his hiring the house dusted and cleaned that one time. And he never offered any. He just got up every morning and went to his job at the car parts factory beneath the clock tower. He worked on an assembly line where he didn't have to make small talk with anyone.

The many secret horrors of my life walked with me every day. The fear of being hated or talked bad about or lied about was kept alive each time I heard the gossips talking. I stayed out of their range of notice as much as I could.

As I got older, I became forgotten in Ardenville, as only the shunned can be forgotten. I was a leper without a colony. I never married or had a girl friend. There was a girl I once liked, but she never knew it. I had no children. My life was on hold, and I knew it. And I was bitter about it, even though I kept it that way on purpose.

In later years, I became an emotional vagrant with a gas station for a home. When I took over Old Bill Addison's gas station and garage out on the edge of Ardenville, thankfully, the gossips still found me too dull and homely to have a life they could talk about.

The garage stood on the edge of town, surrounded by bare fields. There wasn't much traffic out that way, bad for business, but it suited me just fine. I didn't worry about the money. I was already writing car manuals and getting paid for it. People had to come out that way on purpose, and it felt real good to get away from Main Street and all the busybodies that congregated there.

I went to work at old Bill's garage full time, fixing cars and pumping gas after I graduated from high school. I worked there regular for two years before I bought the garage on time from him. There were two other garages in town. I was a natural mechanic though, and people accepted me as I was, because I could keep their cars and trucks in good running condition. At night, I wrote the car manuals.

When I bought the garage, I drove over to the bank in Stoverton to take care of the money end of the business. I wasn't one who bought anything too flashy or extra because I didn't want people asking questions. I was hungry after I got done banking. I was feeling good about the amount of book money I had in the bank, though I didn't know what I would ever use it on.

I went into the little cafe close to the bank and ordered a couple of cheeseburgers to go. I planned on setting in my 1930 black Chevrolet to eat the burgers. Joe Smith and me had fixed it up when I was seventeen. I wasn't in school anymore and didn't have to put up with people. I was damned glad of it. I never liked to stay cooped up inside any place with people very long. I sat down at the counter and waited on my order and stared at the big road map tacked on the wall behind the counter. It had red thumbtacks in it here and there. The young high school waitress with her blond ponytail noticed me staring at it.

"The thumbtacks mark all the places the people are from who stop and eat here."

I didn't answer. I studied the map some more. When my cheeseburgers were ready, the waitress handed me the greasy white paper bag. I asked her where the map came from.

"Next door. At the Stoverton Travel Agency."

She cracked her gum loudly and looked me up and down. I wore my usual navy blue gas station coveralls. She looked away.

"They are pricey, though."

I nodded and left.

I got in the habit of sleeping on a cot in the little back room behind the garage office, even though there was the big house on the corner of Main and Green Street to go home to. The little back room used to be a storeroom. There was a small, high window near the ceiling and a back door leading out to a little strip of scattered gravel and high weeds with a row of some kind of leafy trees behind them. I kept the door to the back room locked.

The year I bought the garage, I was five foot eight, stocky with straight, thick brown hair I kept covered with a grease jockey's cap. My eyes were brown, and I had regular features, just like everybody else. I bathed regular, ate regular, kept my hair cut, bought my clothes on sale at Domart, wore coveralls to work in, and minded my own business.

On the surface, all looked well, but I was never able to face a day of my life with Equanimity. That's what the Zen books I secretly read said I didn't have. I read books all the time, and I learned that Equanimity meant psychological composure and stability. To not be disturbed by the pain I was never been able to explain. To enjoy evenness of mind. To be neither elated nor depressed.

Equanimity meant a person stays even keeled no matter what happens to them. They don't get off kilter. Their minds can stay balanced. They are not disturbed no matter what. But I already knew about the world out there, and I was absolutely terrified of it. I also felt the unseen world out there that couldn't be explained, and I was terrified of that too. I had no passion or yearning past working on old cars and engines and reading the Zen books I was secretly collecting. They were safe.

When I took over the garage, I took down the faded little map Old Bill kept pinned up on the garage office wall and replaced it with the big map I bought over in Stoverton. Old Bill told me that a little kid stopped by now and then to study the map. He called her Map Girl.

I felt a little better after I tacked the new map up on the wall. At least there was a map of some place more than Ardenville for the Map Girl and me to look at if she ever came back. After awhile, I took down the old sign and nailed up a new one that read "Bud's Garage." That's what I went by. Bud. Not Junior, after my father.

The big map was up awhile when Map Girl stopped by to look at it again. I guess she was on her way home from school. She started stopping by every few days to stare at the map, and I made sure I stayed outside in the garage bay where people could see me working on a car. I didn't want any trouble. She caught on and stood just inside the office door by the big front window where everybody could see her. She washed her hands in the sink before she touched the map. I nodded at her for doing that.

A long time passed, and the town didn't seem to notice or say anything. I began to wonder why she wanted to look at the map. What was she seeing or looking for? Maybe the changes and chances this world offered in another town, another place? I looked her over. She was just a plain, pale, brown haired, skinny little kid that didn't talk. We shared that part in common. The not talking part. I bet nobody liked her either. But Map Girl shined with Goodness or something like that, and I could see it in her. She knew I could see it. That's how we started out.

I kept the door to the back room of the garage locked and kept buying and reading books about finding my Equanimity. None of the books made a lick of sense to me on the start, but then something in me was glad I was reading them, so I pushed on. After awhile, I began to catch on to a few things. Evidently, what I was going through and needing had been chased after down through time, and some answers were found, but basically, nobody knew jack about it. It was all up to the person. Well, it all came down to the same thing for me. Not enough veils to hide the reality of life.

Since I banked over in Stoverton to keep the busybodies in Ardenville from knowing anything more about me than they already did, I got the books and other stuff I read sent to my post office box over there. I kept a different bank account in Ardenville for the garage and the old house I grew up in.

When the snow falls just right, it rims the windows people look out of with white.

Ćhapter Two

My father was a Stoic. I learned that word from the Zen books I studied. He wasn't a spiritual Stoic, he was just a plain, everyday Stoic. He did not have Equanimity. He didn't need it. He couldn't be stirred with a stick. He passed away in an ornery mood with a heart attack right after dinner one night. I don't blame him. The homemade sauerkraut he served us was way too salty.

He wasn't an old man or a bad man. He died too young. The few people that came to the funeral said that to me. I nodded and never said anything. But I knew that my father had always been old. I heard the whispers of how much like him I was. I looked up the whispered words. Irascible. Obtuse. Simple. I already knew the meaning of simple. Old and taciturn before my time. Boring and odd, no life. No family or girlfriends or pals. And my mother ran away from us, back to the home in the city she was born in. That proved to me that what they whispered about us was true.

I'd been sleeping in the back room of the gas station for going on three years when father died. I didn't want to go after my mother or find her to tell her he was gone, and she could come home now. I figured she wouldn't come back anyway. I'd put two and two together time and again and it still made four. She didn't like my father and she didn't like me.

I was like my father, and I never changed enough to go and find her and try to start over. Still, sometimes I wondered if her hair was still glossy brown or if anybody else liked her apple pies as much as I did, so I went through the papers she left behind that my father never threw away. I went through them and found an address, wrote down all I knew about her, and went on to Philadelphia to find her. No one knew her at old her home address. The house was old and big, filled knee deep with young married tenants with babies and little kids running all over the place. I got away as quick as I could and went back to the motel room I'd rented. The next morning, as soon as the city offices opened, I went through their records and found her. She was in a cemetery out on Morton Road. She died a year after she run away from home. I ordered a copy of the death certificate. Then I found a general store and bought a pretty yellow gravy bowl, a fine white lace tablecloth, and a jar of pickled pig hocks at a grocery store. I pushed myself through it quick as I could so I wouldn't quit before I got it done.

I put the stuff in my car and drove to the Morton cemetery. It was a big city cemetery, filled with lots of folks crammed up against each other like in an underground subway. I found mother's plot in the pauper's corner of the cemetery and walked backward to it holding the stuff I bought in my hands, hiding it in case she still didn't like me. Which I figured she didn't and never would. I took the fine lace tablecloth out of its package, shook it out, and turned real quick and layered it snowy white over her long, narrow grave. Then I turned my back to her again, set the jar of pickled pig hocks, another one of her favorite things, in the cheerful yellow bowl and turned back around. I placed it careful right where her heart might be to tell her I loved her even if she never liked me. Then I took off. Went home. Tried to forget about it. Got busy.

The old house on Main Street never changed. I wanted to get somebody in to clean it and take my father's things away, but I didn't want anybody carrying stories about the house or me around Ardenville. So I did it myself, a piece at a time. I didn't mind. I was glad to get rid of the smell of Ancient Spice and Avalon Skin Oil. I hated those smells and always will. They make me think of stubbornness and mean, hidden things.

I boxed and bagged up his things and carried them to the Salvation Army over in Stoverton a little bit at a time. There was a Goodwill in Ardenville, but I didn't want to come across anybody wearing his clothes. They weren't much good, and I wanted them far away from me. Everything he left behind went. A piece or a bag at a time; in little bits, so it wouldn't be noticed by neighbors. Living on the corner of Main Street was like living in a goldfish bowl. Everybody watched everybody else and had something to say about them.

I got rid of the dishes we ate off of when he was alive. Then I set out the dishes my mother left behind in the china cabinet. The dishes were dusty, so I washed them careful. They were white with pretty flowers on them. Hidden behind them was a tiny music box with nothing in it. I looked it over and decided to keep it. I wish she'd wanted me, but I could see why she didn't. I took after my father.

The house was filled with creaks and groans and old memories. It was too big, so I closed off the upstairs and used just the downstairs. I did it by going up there and moving my stuff downstairs into the parlor, then going back up there and closing the doors. Father couldn't open them again this time.

I kept every bit of the house dusted. I called the Salvation Army over in Stoverton after a while to come in and carry off my father's empty furniture. It was cheap stuff. Dark and tall and looming, like him. They got to the house at nine in the morning, just after everybody was gone to work, and the gossips were out shopping. I planned it that way. When I called them, I asked them to bring at least four people so they could get the job done in a half hour. They did. I told them to be quiet about it and quick. They were. Nothing got said around town. I took that to mean people never noticed anything.

It didn't matter where I lived, I would have to keep to myself because I was trying to learn how to control what the books I read called my "Shadow" self. I figured I would be mean to others if give a chance, like father was to mother, so I made sure I never took that chance. I stayed as invisible as I could. When people tried to make fun of me or find out things about me, I turned a careful, blank face to them. If they got too heavy handed or insistent about it, I walked away. I'd already made up my mind that I would have to learn from books and not from people. Sometimes I brought a few books back to the house. I picked them up in Stoverton at my mailbox and packed them into plain, brown cardboard boxes labeled car parts, and put them on the backseat of the car. If a neighbor happened to be outside when I took a box out of the car, I just nodded at them and went on in the house.

I carried the boxes in the house and into the locked bedroom on the first floor at the back of the house. Just in case somebody needed to come in the house for some reason. I didn't want them to see any of the kind of books I stored in the house. They would report that I was nuts back to the gossips and trouble might start. Like looney bin stuff.

I wanted them to think I only read car fix it manuals like I kept down at the garage. I ordered books and magazines about Zen and Buddhism and the Dao, and the car fix it manuals I needed to do my work.

The car manuals went on the shelves in back of what I called the "pay me" counter at the garage. The magazines got stacked on the table by the one chair in the office. I locked the rest of the books in the back room of the garage and took a few home now and then for reading when the winter nights got long.

People put up with me because I could fix any car they brought to me. I knew it, and it didn't bother me. I charged a reasonable price for my work. And, I never talked out of school about anything, so they knew I wouldn't spread the gossip going on with folks.

They didn't like me, and that suited me. I was different. I maintained the cool aloofness and the dry neutrality of a horribly shy person while I provided the town's people safe ways to think about me.

Which I was. Beyond shy, I mean. Which I already learned bore its own terrible consequences.

I harbored no ill will or hostility toward anyone. I was too busy trying to survive and fix my fear-filled life. I was forced to stay with keeping my mind on that. Only when I worked on the cars did I feel relief.

"Old Bud," I heard them say.

"He's a loner," they said.

"Bud's crazy over cars, but not over girls."

"Bud's got tinkering with cars on the brain."

"Bud's okay. Boring and dull and simple."

"Bud don't know enough to say anything."

Those were the words the town used to explain me to themselves. Safe, good words.

"Don't bother old Bud, he can barely talk, ha ha!"

"Just leave Bud alone and let him work on our cars and keep them running. He ain't got much to say, but he's the best mechanic in the whole damn state!"

A dendrite is one of four types of snowflakes. It is kin to the stars because it has six points.

Ćhapter Three

Map Girl still stopped by every few days, right after school let out in the afternoon. I made sure I was in the garage working on cars with the doors open, or outside somewhere. If she showed up when I was inside, I stepped out. But nobody seemed to notice her. I could tell she was poor. Once in awhile somebody stopped for gas or to check on a repair when she was there, but nobody seemed to see her. She never said much. Just once, "Can I look at the map?" That was on the start.

"Yup." I answered.

Time went by and Map Girl was growing up. She still stopped by now and then and stared at the map for a while. Then, all of a sudden, she got married to the son of a rounder. Her man was a rounder too. I knew because he stopped for gas now and then. I looked him over and found him to be wanting in anything resembling human decency, even though he was what some people might call handsome. He was slim and medium height with straight blond hair, watchful blue eyes and he wore a cowboy hat and boots. He had a straight, prominent nose and the full, loose lipped mouth of a petted, secret keeping, evil brat pretending to be a good guy. How someone as full of Good as Map Girl got stuck with that no good creep, I don't know. She went straight from her no good family to him. I figured she'd stepped from the frying pan into the fire. It bothered me, but there wasn't anything I could do about it.

She had a little girl pretty quick, and I didn't see her for awhile. Then Map Girl started working at the factory under the clock tower. She always stopped by for gas, regular as clockwork. I always filled the gas tank while she went inside and stared at the map. Then I would step inside and she would pay me. She was always sad, but still full of steady Good and Light.

I was learning about Light from the books I read. That was our weekly routine. One day I said, "Maybe you'll make it out of here someday."

The words come out without me expecting them to or planning them. I watched it when I talked to folks, mostly. She nodded and Light filled her eyes. "I sure hope so," she said, and left. I took up saying that to her every time she stopped for gas so I could see her eyes fill with that same hope and Light.

The years passed. I wrote more car fix it manuals and went over to the bank and my mailbox in Stoverton more often. I got awfully tired of Ardenville, so sometimes I just took a notion to stay the night over there in a good motel. I paid off the garage a few years ago. I would have paid it off sooner, but I didn't want anyone to get suspicious. There was plenty of steady money coming into the bank in Stoverton. Sometimes I thought a little bit about visiting some of the places I was reading about. Katmandu. The Himalayas. England. Stonehenge. Machu Picchu in South America. India. But I stayed still right where I was. In the big old house I was born in on the corner of Green Street and Main, and in my garage. I was afraid to go anywhere else. After awhile, I stopped taking books back to the house. It was too full of Shadows for me to keep them there. I moved them all to the back room of the garage.

The grocery store people knew me, so did everybody else. I listened carefully to the rumors going around about people. I overheard stories about Map Girl and her man. The stories were mixed. Some said he was a fine man, others said he was a bad one, a pervert. All I know is she worked and paid the bills while he ran around. Every time he stopped for gas, he sneered at me because he knew I saw through him. I wanted to hit him bad, but I looked the other way. I could see he was getting worse over time. He stunk of bad thoughts and bad deeds and Elder Spice aftershave. He was one of those whose mother must have taught him to use Old Spruce and other perfumes to disguise his true scent to keep people from smelling his true intentions and knowing what he was.

A lot of people in this old world protect the bad ones, sometimes very cleverly. I read about that in some of my books that told about the ways an evil intended person could disguise their true motives and trap a person. Maybe that's how he got a hold of Map Girl. I figured that's what happened. I could smell his vile, underneath stench and he knew it.

Every time Map Girl stopped for gas, she went inside and stared at the map while her daughter watched me through the car windows with a wistful look on her face. Her girl looked like her, not like him. She had the longest, straightest brown hair I ever saw. Her brows were heavy but light, like sandy colored, curved moth wings. Her large prominent eyes were the color of a Chevrolet Coupe I once liked. They were filled with wariness and Goodness, too, like Map Girl's. I wasn't one to smile at anybody, but I did clean the window she was looking out of until it shined.

Map Girl loved old cars as much as I did. We both liked the old land yachts the best. She'd gone through a couple of them. Over the years, I'd kept them serviced and repaired for her. These days, she was driving a blue and white 1957 Mercury Turnpike Cruiser, one of the real queens of the land yacht world. I fixed a couple of things on it for her and kept it in tip top shape for her.

One day when she paid me for the gas, I said, "Maybe you'll get out of here someday for good," I always added the "for good," now, because I'd heard about her trying to escape him before and not making it.

She said, "My daughter is twelve now."

I took her words and examined them. The nuances in them held something secret, something desperate. I remembered what I heard about her man and children. I nodded and pointed.

"There's the map when you're ready. Make it soon."

She nodded and left.

In a few days she came back. I gassed up her car and went back in the office where she stood staring at the map. She was pale and frightened. I remembered the skinny little brown haired kid she once was.

"How much for the map?" she asked.

I studied her for awhile. I wanted to give it to her for nothing. But I knew better.

"Five dollars."

She nodded and left.

She was leaving this place. Soon. I hoped in a good way. Leaving the stench and filth of that bad man behind. I needed to know if she had enough money to leave here on, that's why I put the high price of five dollars on the map. I knew she'd left him before, but he always hunted her down and brought her back. But now her kid was in danger.

I wanted to offer her money. I wanted her to get away for good this time and never come back. I was making plenty of money, more coming in all the time, but I couldn't figure out a way to give her any money and still protect myself.

I made a quick trip over to Stoverton and drew out a big wad of cash just in case I figured out how to get it to her, and bought a new map. I took them back to the gas station and hid them in the back room. Then I waited.

Map Girl stopped for gas one morning. It was the day after school let out. She looked all steamed up and desperate. I stuffed the wad of cash in my back coveralls pocket and went out to gas up her car while she went inside and stared at the map. I knew Map Girl often went off on blissful misconceptions of what a dollar could buy. Her daughter was sitting in the Mercury's backseat on the passenger side. She scooted over to the window and watched me solemnly. We were acquainted by now, and I nodded at her.

The talk was her kid was bossy and moody. I'd already deduced that she was like me, in that she learned the hard way early to put up a front to keep people away so as to get by in this world. That was why she was moody. Doing that made her old for her age. With her father, no doubt she was forced to.

She was already taller than her mama, who was about four inches shorter than me. I figured they neither one would ever put much weight on, for they were too touchy and nervous for that. Somehow, I knew this would be the last time I saw them. The pressure inside me kept building while I tried every way in hell to figure out a way to get the money to Map Girl so she could finally make a successful get away.

I washed the windshield and all the side windows while Map Girl's daughter watched me. After I got her window done, she rolled it down. On the front seat, passenger side, sat a giant carpet bag. I grabbed the wad of money out of my back pocket, reached past her through her window, and shoved the money down into the carpet bag. She watched me and didn't say a word.

"Don't tell her," I said.

She nodded.

"I'll hide it."

I nodded in agreement. Evidently we both knew Map Girl's way with money. Those ways had kept her dependent too long on that sorry excuse for a man. She reached over the seat and into the carpet bag, pulled the wad of money out, and stuffed it into her jeans pocket. Then, real quick, she told me a couple things to do with a couple people in town. Unfinished business, she called it. I gave her one last, long look, and strolled back inside, trying to calm my breathing down.

Map Girl handed me five dollars and carefully took the map down herself. Patiently, she folded it until it became a small square. Then she stared at me and started to say something. I watched the hope and fear cross her face.

I cut it short.

"Better get going," I said.

She grabbed me and gave me a quick hug before she run out to the Mercury, opened the trunk, and hid the map under the carpet lining. Then she jumped in the Mercury, waved at me, and took off without looking back. Her girl stared at me through the back window until they were out of sight.

I went in the back room, got out the identical new map I was saving just in case, and put it up exactly where the old one was. I didn't want her man or anyone else to come in here and see the map gone. It was none of their damn business.

Sure enough, her man come around and asked me if I'd seen her. I looked him straight in the eye and told him I didn't know a damn thing about it. He started to bluster and try to bully me. I never wanted to hit anyone so bad in my life and almost did. I wanted to demolish him, so he didn't walk the face of the Earth anymore. He saw that in me and backed right off and walked away real quick. He got in his car and took off like the devil was after him. Maybe he didn't know it, but I already knew the devil had a hold of him. He'd pay some day. He would find out just how much when the time come right. I'd read plenty about that in my books on karma and how it worked. Her man never came around for gas again. I figured he read the handwriting on the wall real clear and figured out he would most likely get his ass stomped if he ever showed up here again.

I was in my early thirties the summer Map Girl and her daughter left Ardenville and never came back. Months passed after they left. Fall passed, then winter set in. I kept to my usual habits of work and more reading. About seven months went by. Then one day, the phone at the garage rang. When I answered it, a man's voice told me where they were, then Map Girl got on the phone and cried and said she loved me. I asked her where she was, and she told me. I told her she would always be my little Map Girl. Then she hung up. It was a hasty, quick call, but one I didn't forget.

I'd wondered many times if Map Girl and her daughter landed in a good place. I'd speculated on many a good ending on their behalf. That's what the energy books said was the Good thing to do. I knew Map Girl was some kind of angel. She'd just been taken hostage for awhile by the evil that lived in Ardenville, but not for forever. That was the good part.

Dendrites are tiny fractal trees...

Chapter Four

Then, after more years passed, a private detective came to town to check up on Map Girl's husband. The detective's name was Dan Swain. He was stocky with light brown hair and bushy brows, a square, jolly face with a wide mouth, and big ham hands he used all the time to help him explain his words. After we got to know each other, we both laughed at his name.

Dan tried to be subtle on the start. He stopped at the garage one day. He was driving a beat up, ragged 1950 Ford, two door tan sedan. He parked his car by the garage bay where I was working on a car. He got out, shut his door, and mopped his face off with the biggest, whitest handkerchief I have ever seen. It wasn't very hot out, but he was mopping his face like it was the hottest day of summer. I guessed he was under some kind of stress. I stopped what I was doing and waited. He gestured at the Ford.

"Damn car's got something wrong with it. I don't know what. It keeps dying on me."

I pulled the Ford into one of the two garage bays and opened the hood. I didn't mind the sunshine. It was just easier to work in the shady, cooler bay.

He stood around and asked questions about the car and Ardenville while I tinkered under the hood. Being one who didn't have much to say to anybody at any time, I just plain didn't answer.

When I was satisfied that I could find nothing wrong with his car, I closed the hood.

"No charge," I said.

There was something wrong here, and I didn't want to know what it was. Who was he looking to get in trouble with his questions? I wanted him to leave. I stared at him and waited.

"Okay," he said, shrugging. "You got me. Map Girl sent me."

Elation washed over me. Map Girl. He knew her name. So she made it this far, this long. A few years had gone by without word from her. I haven't loved many people in my life. But I loved Map Girl. I loved her Light. The Goodness in her. She was a lost one who made it out of here. I stared at the ground a minute to steady myself. Then I grabbed a rag and went to rubbing the dust off the hood of his car to cover my feelings. A car drove in and stopped in front of the gas pumps. I turned my back to him and spoke over my shoulder.

"Come back at seven tonight. I close at six."

He got in his car and left without a word. I gassed up the car waiting at the pumps. They paid me and drove off. I went inside the office, turned the closed sign to the window front, closed the door and locked it. I sat down on the cheap black fake leather chair behind the counter and studied the map on the wall. I took my time and studied it over. Old Bill's little map was tacked up there first, then my big one. Map Girl's map. Then the new map that was turning old over the years. This one was mine.

I wished I'd thought to ask Old Bill before he passed away as to why he put his map up on the garage office wall. Was he once a big thinker with a little map, hoping he might leave this place too? Then I started to worry. I wondered if Map Girl was okay. I would find out tonight.

I thought about life, how it rushed by like a river moving too fast. In between the years I heard from Map Girl, I'd made a couple of friends. Ben and Andy. Ben Bass and Andrew Noble. They were like I was, but none of us talked about that part of our selves.

Ben and Andy were labeled oddballs in grade school. Like me, they'd gone unnoticed by the people in Ardenville all of their lives. It didn't take me long to figure out they made sure it went that way, just like I did. On purpose.

Map Girl was gone about three years when Andy and Ben showed one Saturday morning at the gas station. They were riding in a rusty 1952 Chevy station wagon needing a lot of work. That's how I met them. It was pouring down rain that day. I was working on a transmission in one of the bays. They parked Andy's long land yacht to the side of the garage, got out and closed their doors without slamming them. I noticed they parked out of the way, a discreet and respectful thing to do. Something I did. Automatically.

Most people thought nobody noticed you unless you parked right smack in front of them. It was rude and uncalled for to me, but most people liked to push themselves on to others. I didn't want to push or be pushed on. Neither one. I just wanted to stay out of the way of the flow of mainstream madness. Customers sometimes pulled right up in front of the garage bay doors and let their car die right there. I've pushed a few rude, dumb people's cars out of the way so I could get a fixed car out of the bay, paid for, and on its way.

*

Mornings have always been my worst times. I wake up in this world with a sinking feeling of doom every morning without fail. It wasn't anything like I didn't want to be here. I didn't want to be there either. Wherever there was. I held no hankering to move to a desert island or to a mountain top so I would be happier, like people wanted to do. I already figured out that I was going to stay the way I was no matter where I got planted. I didn't like Ardenville. But I also didn't have a clue as to where else I was supposed to be.

The books said I was supposed to be exactly where I was, but I knew better. I lived a miserable life that nobody else seemed to want. At least I never heard any rumors to the contrary. I tried making rituals up to get through the mornings. Any ritual to do every morning to help myself. I made tea for awhile. I read that getting up and getting dressed and the rest of it were what the books called the mundane rituals of life. None of them worked for me. The astrology books I researched said I was probably born at a bad time. I agreed. I was flat footed too.

I aspired to meditation, but that didn't last long, for mites have been eating on me for most of my life. Dust mites, eyelash mites, book mites, pollen mites. You name them, any kind of mites. Constant showers and changes of clothes keep them down enough for me to survive. I'm damned allergic to them and a whole bunch of other things. I think it probably all started with being allergic to my parents, and other people and things just snowballed from there.

Most people don't notice I have allergies since I wear coveralls and have some grease somewhere on me most of the time because of the garage. Which is where they mostly see me. There and the grocery store. I noticed a long time ago that people don't like to get too close to regular dirt, so I keep a little bit on me for protection. Besides, I never have much to say anyway.

The books say I am a Sensitive in disguise. Anyways, the older I get, the more I get the sinking moods. I get better after noon, but it comes back on me about six o'clock and seven in the evening. That's when I have to have dinner by myself and endure loneliness openly again. Everybody's living through their own kind of hell I guess.

Anyway, Ben and Andy hurried into the bay and turned their backs to me and stared out at the rain. They both wore black rimmed glasses. Ben's lenses were thin, but Andy looked like he was looking at the world through the bottom of Coke bottles. They took their glasses off, cleaned them and put them back on. Then they glanced at me and looked back out into the rain.

They didn't seem to be inclined to try to hurry me, so just for the hell of it, I stopped working on the transmission. The steady rain had made me more lonesome than usual. I put the tools down and washed my hands off. I didn't ask what the matter was with the station wagon. Instead, I offered them a cup of hot raspberry tea with a slice of dried pineapple in it just to see what they would say.

They blinked at me like two owls.

"Sounds good," they finally answered in unison.

"Wait here," I ordered them.

I went in the office, unlocked the back room, slipped in, and retrieved the hot plate and the tea pot. I plugged it in behind the pay me counter. Then I grabbed two more cups out of the back room and locked it up again.

Ben and Andy. I mulled over what I'd heard about them while I made the tea. They didn't try to follow me into the office. That was good. Give us all some breathing room.

Ben and Andy were talked about in Ardenville in the same way I was. Both of them were born here. They'd been friends since childhood. The gossips said they were odd ducks. Nobody could figure them out. My guess was nobody was ever interested enough to try. Just like me. No marriages, no children, no law degrees. Just mechanical engineering degrees. They lived at opposite ends of town in small rent houses. In their spare time, Andy fished and Ben read science fiction books.

They both worked at the factory under the clock tower in the middle of town, designing car parts. They made good money and kept to themselves. They refused to attend any of the churches in town. They refused to sit on the City Council. Both of them came from big families that raced past them to make the front page gossip in the Ardenville Gazette.

I liked that they never followed me inside. I poured them full mugs of hot raspberry tea and added dried pineapple slices to sweeten it, just like I did for myself, and carried it out to them. I never liked coffee or regular store bought tea, so I made my tea from dried fruits. I kept a dehydrator back at the house I dried fruits and other stuff on. I run it during the day, and it made the old place smell less musty and not lived in at night.

We stood together and drank tea and watched the rain fall. None of us said anything. What can a person dedicate their entire existence to? Those two guys dedicated it to their tea and the rain and me and each other for as long as it lasted. Then we did a little car talk.

Later on that night, before I drifted off to sleep, I realized the three of us had shared a Zen moment, like my books described. These were polite, practical, scared to death of life, Zen men, lonely like me, and we just sort of drifted together.

I learned over time that Ben liked to read science fiction to keep himself alert to the awful possibilities' life might bring. He knew about the Shadow too. Andy liked to fish, but not to catch anything. He needed water, but the waves made him sick and the fish smells revolted him. It was where he went to avoid his Shadow, so he paid the price required. That's what I learned about them. Enlightenment. We all sought it. Because we thought that's how we didn't have to come back here. That's how we got out of here. Ha! Supposedly. Yeah, I wasn't buying that for one minute.

Goodness and Kindness seeped from Ben and Andy. That was enough for me. We became friends. I had friends for the first time. Not one, but two of them. All of our Shadows were attachments who knew we didn't know jack about attachment yet. We didn't, or we would have held a silent protest outside of town in a field somewhere to scare the Shadows off. Due to the Shadows we carried, we sure as hell knew what steady, stark fear was, though. We lived with it daily. Fear was the glue holding our miserable little lives together.

Then we discovered a second glue that held us three together. Bowling. We all liked to bowl, though I barely knew how to on the start. There was a bowling alley down by the high school, but we didn't go there. Too many people we knew. Too many winos, ex jocks, and people who thought religion and being married with a nagging spouse and bratty children was the path of the correct and righteous on their way to Heaven, which we knew such place was involved with constant cases of mistaken identity on God's part.

We went bowling over in Summit instead. Summit was a small town about twenty miles away. Andy and Ben had been bowling over there on Wednesdays and Thursdays at two o'clock in the afternoons for a long time. That's the days and times the old folks with no memories left, bowled. We didn't bother them and they never bothered us. They acted like we were okay. They didn't know or remember us every week. They forgot our names regular as clockwork every three weeks. That satisfied us real good.

We drank a few beers and ate greasy, tasty cheeseburgers, laughed a little bit, and never stayed past five o'clock in the afternoon. Never entered our minds to push it by staying later. We couldn't. It would have been too much.

Life wasn't fair, but we stayed away from that fact because we knew being "fair" usually involved some form of retribution involving having to live the skimpy lives we were living. There was no sense of purpose to any of it. The three of us knew it and accepted it and went bowling and thought about land yachts. We bowled through the summer and the fall, then winter came.

Snowfall's density is determined by visibility.

Çhapter Five

It snowed a lot in the winter in Ardenville. That was a blessing, if you want to get religious about it. Us three counted on the promise of snow in Ardenville. I was crazy about snow. It was the best thing to happen in Ardenville all year. Every year the town got blanketed in good, peaceful white snow for months. While it was snowing, magic happened. The sharp, mean town sounds were muted. The streetlights shone soft and dim without summer's hard glare. The old gossips had arthritis and stayed in mostly while the younger ones were kept busy with their kid's extra needs. They had to warm up their cars before they could go places, and they had to pay attention to the icy or snowy streets instead of staring at people's porches and windows, trying to see something that wasn't none of their business. Many of the experts at taking some innocent thing and making something bad out of it were out of commission most of the winter.

When I was growing up, I watched the snow coming down through my bedroom window and then through the living room window after my father died. By that time, when the gossips drove by, I knew they wouldn't notice me. I wasn't of interest to them. When I was a kid, I went out in the backyard and hid behind the bushes and played in the snow. I held secret conversations with the snow. I told it about wanting my mother to come to the back door and call my name loud with missing me, and order me to come in, saying she'd made yeast raised glazed sweet rolls for me and there was hot chocolate to go with them. Or she had hot chicken noodle soup waiting just for me.

She knew what I was doing, what I waited for the first snow to do. I stuck my tongue out and gathered snowflakes on it, tasting, making sure they were real. Then I talked my guts out to the snow coming down. All the words I stored up through spring, summer, and fall and wouldn't share with her, poured out like an undammed river. I hemmed them up inside me, waiting for snow to fall each year. The snow carried my miseries away until I felt peaceful. Balanced. Without any fear, at least for a short time. The snow's silence was stronger when it became bitter cold and the ground snow sparkled like diamonds.

After I talked myself out, I was able to play awhile. I pretended I had a friend and we would build a snow fort together and throw snowballs at the tree in the corner by the bushes, but never at each other. Then my mother would actually call me in for hot chocolate and a homemade, yeast raised, glazed sweet roll. I would look at her and she would look at me and smile. I smiled back and let her hold my hands. But I never let her have my words, let her be my savior. Because my father wouldn't have stood for it. So that's as far as it went. Still, she made the best sweet rolls I have ever tasted. I remember and miss the sweetness of them when snow falls.

The house stayed silent the rest of the year. Then mother ran away from us. Father ignored my jaunts into the falling snow after she left. I hid under the elm tree and cried out my pain into the snowflakes falling around me. They helped me manage to survive that first winter without her.

I walked to school in the snow and watched the other kids playing in it with sleds and things. I stayed out of their way and off to the side, but I liked watching them play in the snow. I carefully observed them; their sleds versus toboggans and what each one did, their saucers and how to make them go faster down hills, gloves versus mittens, earmuffs versus scarves, versus hats, coats, snow pants, socks, all of it, and learned.

By the time fall came and the leaves started turning, I was having a pretty good time with Ben and Andy, my first friends, and now I trusted them a little more. It would take time, but we were learning each other.

Time passed and I grew restless. I got so I wanted to do more than hide out in Ardenville and bowl over in Summit once a week. It wasn't enough. I got to thinking about winter. It would be on us before we knew it. And it would last a long time. Winter came early and stayed late in these parts. I studied out what to do. The garage bays were heated, so that wasn't a problem. I could work all I wanted to. There were no other calls on my time, except for going bowling. I loved nature and needed it. Always did. Always would. I had a long standing habit of going on long rides away from Ardenville so I could think things out and keep a good perspective, so I knew the country around here pretty well. There was a national forest that started about ninety miles north of Ardenville. I got so I liked to drive up there to think and relax. Nature always did that for me.

One fall afternoon when I was up by the forest riding around, I chanced upon a small lake I didn't know was there. I drove around it until the road thinned down into an unused trail. When I turned around, I noticed a few old cabins on the other side of the lake. I drove back around the lake and looked them over. There were a couple of cabins that had been empty for a long time. One of them had a for sale sign taped to a dusty front window.

I didn't think any more about it until my tax man over in Stoverton told me I better spend some of my book money, or the government would take it away from me. Well, I sure didn't want them to have it. That's when I bought the cabin. First, I went back up to the lake and looked over all the cabins around the lake. Each one was a good distance apart, separated by a quarter of a mile, thick with trees. I chose the one with the faded for sale sign. It needed some repair, but it looked like it had been tended to not too long ago. I went up and looked at it three times and once in the rain to make sure I liked it before I took Ben and Andy up there with me. I told them we were just going for a ride.

"What about this place?" I asked to them as we drove past it. "Want to look at it?"

We stopped and got out. They inspected the place, stick by stick, almost.

Finally Andy said, "You can't fool us. You thinking about buying it?"

They both peered at me in the early afternoon sun.

"I don't know," I answered cautiously. "What do you boys think about it?"

"Well, we like it all right, but it looks like your big footprints are already back there behind the cabin."

I grinned.

"Yep."

I did have big feet. Some folks called that a better understanding. They looked at each other. Andy spoke decisively while Ben nodded in agreement.

"Well, we're in. We like getting away from Ardenville too. It will be good to have a place to go to. We'll each put in a third on buying it. But we don't want anybody else to know about it. It will be our secret cabin, okay guys?"

"Absolutely."

We all said it solemnly together and chuckled. A chuckle was damn close to a laugh. That pleased us.

We cleaned the place up and stayed there a few times overnight. I racked my brain for an acceptable excuse to give people so I could take time off from the garage without them getting curious. I finally just didn't say anything. I took down the old sign and put up a new notice. A small, hand printed paper taped on the office door window reading, "Open Tuesday, Wednesday, & Thursday 7 to 2," in black print on white. That gave me four days off each week for a long weekend.

We started going up to the cabin to get some rest from our organized, boring lives. We felt like we'd already lived through every bad book plot ever written before we showed up this lifetime. We were all tired and jacked out of shape. We needed the cabin and all that went with it. Freed from prying eyes and gossip, we expanded and relaxed and fixed the place up suitable for three bachelors. We bought snowmobiles. Andy fished, Ben hunted, and we set around and drank a little beer. It felt awful good to get out of Ardenville for a few days each week.

Around Christmas, Ben and Andy were on mandatory vacation time from their jobs because the factory was closed. I closed the garage, and we spent more than a week up at the cabin. Now you might ask what we talked about. I soon discovered that we were all masters of hiding behind our defenses. Nobody was going to get behind them. Each other, either. Andy and Ben had been friends all of their lives. There was a part of themselves that already knew how to make at least one friend. I never learned it. They worked hard to pull me in. It took some doing before we talked about ourselves to each other. No blabby, spill your guts stuff, just a dry remark now and then, deliberately thought up and presented for the others to ponder on.

The easy part was that all three of us were crazy about snow. Any kind of snow. Any time. Everybody in town complained all damn winter about the cold and snow. I got tired of hearing it.

They stayed bitter about it snowing for nine months out of the year, ten some years, so we never said a word to any of them about liking winter better than anything. We discovered that each of us, early on in our youth, decided we'd just have to put up with the rest of the seasons.

We liked winter because it seemed to make our fears cast a smaller Shadow. Maybe it froze them or shrunk them up. Snow brought us relief from our Shadows. When we were up at the cabin, we tiptoed together through the smaller Darkness that winter offered. Three middle aged, terrified old men that the Shadows in life kept bullied and scared down to a whisper of Being. Old men, not bothering anybody, just surviving.

To be with another survivor was new and enough. We each bore solitary natures, but we sensed that with each other, we might have a better social life. Any social life. With each other, our Shadows might dim down into a manageable size. My Zen books said it took a collective of people to make that happen. That it was impossible to accomplish with just one or two. The books said it was the unconscious parts of people that compelled us to make friends. Well, we found out it took at least three. That sounds pretty damn poetic, but it's true, and the only way I know how to put it.

*

By the time I met Dan Swain, Map Girl's hired detective, me and Andy and Ben had been going up to the cabin for a couple of years. I was going to be cautious with him because he was a detective and he sure as hell wasn't going to get anything out of me about the cabin or Map Girl.

Dan Swain came back at seven like I asked him to. He was right on time. That was good. Not too early, so he could catch me off guard and snoop around. The garage bay doors were open, and I was tinkering under a car hood to provide a cover for myself when he got there.

He parked around the side of the garage and strolled in like he wasn't up to anything. He peered under the hood of the rusty blue De Soto and offered an opinion on the new fangled lights.

"Those damn power pop up headlights have caused De Soto a hell of a lot of trouble! Had one myself for awhile. Got too many miles on it. Had to get rid of it."

He grinned and shrugged.

"Yeah, the headlights are a big problem," I said.

"You have to order them?"

"Yep. And wait awhile before they get here. I'm wondering what's on your mind. I'm waiting on that too."

"Can we go in your office and talk?" He looked around apologetically. "I don't want somebody to accidentally hear us."

I closed the De Soto's hood and shut the bay doors. The closed sign was in already place in the front window of the garage office. The front door was locked. It was coming on full dark, and I left the office light off. He didn't ask why. There was just enough dusk left to see.

"Make it quick, I don't want anybody connecting me to Map Girl for her own protection," I ordered.

"Her daughter Geena has married, and she is going to have a baby. Map Girl wants to know what her husband is up to so she can protect her daughter and the baby from him. She hired me to find out everything I can about him, and then I am to do regular checkups and report to her on him every six months. Is he still among the living?" he asked me.

"Yep. And that's too damn bad," I stated.

He showed me his credentials and handed me a folded note Map Girl sent him to give me. The paper crackled as I opened and read her permission slip asking me to tell him all I could. That's how we got started. Six months later, Dan Swain was back in Ardenville again. After that it was too risky, he'd been in town too many times, and someone might get suspicious. I met him over in Stoverton.

By that time, Ben and Andy knew about Dan. I wanted them to meet him. I also wanted their help in filling out the picture on Map Girl's husband. We snooped around and found out that Map Girl's ex divorced her so he could remarry jailbait. An only child from a rich farm family. The next time we met with Dan at our cabin. We met there from then on.

Dan had some of the worst habits I ever seen. He was as jumpy as anything. He carried a handgun with a long barrel in a custom tooled leather holster. The barrel was so long he couldn't bend over easy when he carried it.

Dan wore a little, sandy colored mustache. He said he wore it to disguise himself from the women who were always after him. His hair was thin and sandy colored. His eyes were tiny, lively, little, and brown, kind of like a squirrel's eyes. His teeth were large, white and even in his wide mouth. His nose was squat nose and buckled at the tip. Dan would eat anything.

Day old cheeseburgers and stale donuts were favorites of his. I stayed afraid he would get food poisoning and die of it. Ben and Andy made friends with Dan instantly. They helped fill in the rest of the picture for the Map Girl Reports. That's what we named them.

Dan started coming to the cabin for a long weekend every six months. Sometimes the weekend stretched into a week or more. The four of us fished and hunted and roamed around the woods and fired up the old grill out in back of the cabin.

Dan said he always had a bunch of girlfriends, but none ever stuck. He was as old as us and never been married. He had a bunch of kids, though. One or two by this girl, one or two by another girl. And more still by another girl. He was kid poor. Every extra dime he earned beyond survival went toward child support.

I admired that he was happy and never complained about his threadbare existence because he couldn't keep it in his pants. At least his women weren't jailbait. They were mature women who still loved him madly, and liked each other, too. Or so he said.

Andy and Ben teased him about using condoms.

"I do now...that it's too late!" He exclaimed ruefully.

"But them women, they're crazy about me! They get carried away with me, and tear 'em right off of me. They're after them good genetics I carry! They wanna' make babies from me and pass 'em on!"

Dan told me about Map Girl's new life and where the little store was in New Mexico. Maybe I will do something someday with what he told me. Maybe I'll go visit Map Girl and her daughter and meet that good man Dan said she found out there. Maybe I will drop in and see if Map Girl still remembers me.

Dan visited us and made reports for another five years or so. Then Map Girl's ex-husband died after a long, drawn out struggle with cancer. I heard the details from Andy whose mother attended the big, elaborate funeral. There was a horse drawn glass carriage with his casket inside, drummers, and the works. His mean, tainted young wife went all out, crying and throwing herself on the casket and trying to open it.

Andy knew the hospice workers. They were from over in Sutton. They never liked the man. They said he was one of the most unethical people they ever tended to. They said he stayed angry and surprised and made every effort to get someone else to take the cancer on, to take his place in the death lineup, to give their life up so he could live, but he couldn't find anybody. It wasn't possible, anyway. Finally, he was forced to deal with something he couldn't get away with or control. We were all relieved. Map Girl and her daughter and little granddaughter were safe from him at last. We knew that a lot of other people were safe now, too, especially women and little girls.

Dan wanted to keep on meeting with Ben and Andy and me, so we went on just as we'd been doing. We met at the cabin every six months. Being cautious, we agreed never to tell anyone in Ardenville anything. We still didn't want the rest of Map Girl's ex asshole family to ever know where her and her girl were. It was easier with Map Girl's ex dead. No more reports on him. Except how were we supposed to keep up on what was going on with Map Girl and her family?

Sometimes the universe has a way of converging and making things just right. Our cabin was hidden back in the woods, set snug against a small private lake. The little lake was nestled into a thick ring of trees running right down to the edge of the water. The small lake was filled with fish. Our cabin had two small bedrooms, a front room and a tiny bathroom with a potty, sink, and shower stall in it.

The tax man told me for a second time that I best spend some more of my book money, or the government would take it away from me, so I decided to add a fancy deck to the back of the cabin. That way, nobody could see it, and nobody would know about it. I started drawing up plans for a plain wood deck. Then Andy, Ben, and Dan got in on the act. I got carried away too and added a place for grilling and a picnic table.

The deck kept growing. Dan added an outdoor waterproof sofa. Ben added a retractable rainproof awning over the sofa for when it rained. Andy added a sink for washing fish and a deep fryer for hush puppies, which meant a small stove as well as a huge grill out there.

I said, "Why don't we add a couple of beds, while we are at it?"

"Great idea!"

"I was just joking," I said. They added hammocks instead.

"Instead of putting the hammocks on the deck, how about enclosing the front porch, and putting them out there?" Dan said.

"But that dinky little porch would have to be made bigger," Andy explained. "Much bigger. It would have to be converted into a wraparound."

Everybody fell into a well of silent speculation and stared at me, waiting.

Finally I said, "I don't care, as long as it looks like the rest of the cabin. I don't want it to look new. I don't want nobody to notice anything. I want it to look like it has always been here. And the work has to be done real quick and quiet."

"I'll help pay," Ben said.

"Me too," Andy said.

"We'll take care of your part, Dan. We both got plenty."

"Yeah, Mr. Rockefellers, speak for yourselves!" I said.

"My God, he made another joke!" Ben and Andy laughed.

"That's two this week!"

Dan shrugged and grinned in embarrassment.

"You know how it is," he sighed.

"No we don't Dan, and don't you tell us, either!"

We found a contractor to come in and do everything quick and quiet. Two days, and it would be done. We paid top dollar to get it done in that amount of time, but it was worth it. Dan, Ben, Andy, and me met at the cabin on Friday afternoon. The workers were scheduled to start Saturday morning. We were nervous and excited. I should say Dan was excited. The other three of us were terrified of an unexpected shoe dropping on us, so to speak.

For the first time, we got to wondering about our neighbors. I'd never seen much of anybody around the lake. I guess our neighbors liked to keep to themselves just like we did. But since we needed to know where trouble might come from, we piled into Ben's blue and white 1951 Dodge Royal and circled the lake.

It was the average small lake of eight or ten acres one finds in the north. There were many in this area close to the National forest. I didn't know the Lake had a name until we came across a faded sign that said Lake Gray Heron. A good name. It sounded dignified. Except the "L" and the "N" were missing.

"ake Gray Hero," Dan mused.

"Speak for yourself," Andy said. "We're all older than you, but I got Bayer's Aspirin. So far, they cure any problem."

We wandered the grassy, narrow path passing for a road around the lake, and discovered two falling down cabins, one old camp site, and a small one room travel trailer that was once painted a violent, hopeful lime green. We concluded after our short tour that we were alone at the lake. No wonder we'd only seen a couple of fishermen drive by. Ever. Dan yelped with pleasure. The rest of us just grinned.

The building crew arrived at dawn the next morning. We were up and waiting for them with piles of flapjacks and syrup, sausage, and coffee to fluff them up a bit. None of us were above that sort of bribery. There was a bunch of them, and they were all over the place. No shouting, just hustling and hammering going on.

I kept a lookout for vehicles coming in off the main road and hoped like hell we could get it done without any government people coming by and asking us about permits or such. We none wanted to go to jail over this.

The construction crew worked from dawn until dusk on Saturday. Then they came back Sunday morning at dawn and started up again. We cooked and did what we could to help. We were four old guys, a bit gripey and a little grungy. Three of us, anyway. Dapper Dan was dressed in a tan and orange plaid shirt, khaki shorts, and white tennis shoes. The crew finished at two o'clock on Sunday afternoon. I handed the construction boss his big fat check and they packed up and hurried away. Me and Ben and Andy went up to the cabin over the next three weekends to finish cleaning up the place and put the finishing touches on the new construction. Then we stayed home for awhile. Partly because of work, and partly so we didn't stir up suspicion.

Snow is solidified precipitation. Each snowflake is its own organically organized arrangement.

Ćhapter Six

On Memorial Day, Ben and Andy and I drove up to the cabin. Dan met us there. We planned to stay a few days and try out the new deck and grill and all the other new things. The next morning about eleven o'clock, the four of us old fogies were sitting out on the new deck of the cabin drinking beer and admiring the view over the lake, when the car horns started blowing. Three of us froze in place. Dan fell out of his lawn chair and dropped his beer. It spilled and ran between the boards of the deck. I knew right then that our nice little world had ended.

Ben and Andy and I looked at each other, and all three of us began quaking harder than the aspens they brag about growing in Colorado. Dan didn't look at us. He picked himself up off the deck and ambled into the cabin like nothing was wrong. Like us having company was a normal thing. Andy, Ben, and me stared at each other. We'd been betrayed! Dan didn't look at us even once. He didn't understand us, after all. Well, we had definite rules about betrayals.

This meant Dan had to go. Arriving at that conclusion took only an instant for us. The next instant, car doors slammed and the shouting, happy voices of many children and a few women assaulted our vulnerable, offended ears. We jumped to our feet in horror as the sound of running feet and children's voices and laughter headed toward our sacred cabin.

We had to get out of here! As one, we dropped our beer cans and fled down the back steps of the deck toward the dock. We kept two rowboats tied up at the dock. Andy's boat had a trolling motor on it.

We untied the two rowboats and shoved the one out into the lake and jumped into Andy's boat. He jerked the cord and the engine started. They both looked at me with gratitude. I kept every engine on the place running smooth as butter, and for once, I was damn glad I did.

We purred slowly away from the horror gathering behind us like a thunderstorm of unknown proportions. We watched as three women and a dozen kids aged from first grade through high school delinquents ran to the dock. They waved and shouted and pointed at us. We looked away and purred slowly on across the lake. Andy guided the boat up on a grassy bank on the opposite side of the lake. We got out and trudged into the woods where we couldn't be seen before anyone spoke.

It was time to get rid of Dan. We stared at each other. It was time to move on. Our cover had been blown. There was nothing more to say. The cabin was no longer ours. And Dan knew where we lived in Ardenville.

"It's time for me to go home and retire, leave Ardenville and move on to someplace new," I said.

"Me too." Ben said.

"Me too." Andy said. "We better do it quick before he finds us."

We headed back to the cabin. We trudged slowly and sadly around the lake. When we got close to the cabin, we hid behind trees until we got to our cars.

There was no one around. Evidently, they were still all out by the water. We could hear their voices. We slipped into our cars, started the engines and tore out of there like bats leaving Hell behind.

 We headed for my garage back in Ardenville. We parked our cars in the woods behind the garage. Then we slipped into the garage and locked the doors. It was afternoon, so there was plenty of light. But there was also a large picture window in the office that anybody could see us through.

I unlocked the back room door and ushered Andy and Ben inside. It was the first time anybody else was ever in the back room. I turned on the light and waited while they spun in a slow circle. My fantasy life was no longer hid from them. I planned to hide it from everyone the rest of my life. But sometimes life doesn't turn out the way you planned.

The dark blue, star filled universe above them glowed with life. It was painted on the ceiling by a fine artist from up north the first year I owned the garage. Books filled one wall. First editions, hard bound, dust jackets. Neat and big and shiny books. Bibles. Euclid's Table of Elements, one of the few copies left in existence. Zen books. Zen posters. One of a carb twelve atom. Ballet dancers and Al Jolson singing. A cot in the corner, plain and unadorned. White sheets and a rough green blanket. One pillow covered with a white pillowcase. An ornate cross above the cot. A small rag rug in front of the cot for bare feet to land on. A short dresser. At the back of the room, a table and small white bathroom with a shower, sink and potty.

I shrugged. Customers either pissed out back or went down the road and found another bathroom to use. I plugged the hot plate in and placed the tea pot on it and turned it on. Now what?

Andy spoke first.

"Well, I'm not going back. It's ruined for me now. Even if I went back, it's still over."

Ben and I nodded in agreement.

"We could patch it up, but it's broke."

The horror of a bunch of bossy women and noisy children invading our quiet cabin, our personal, sacred space, made us shudder. None of us liked having anything to do with either of them. Dan knew they were coming. He should have known better. But he didn't understand us. He wasn't afraid of life like we were. He thought the more of it, the merrier. Maybe he thought it would be okay, that when we met them, we would somehow think all of a sudden that they were charming.

It took us two hours to come up with a plan. When we were ready, we piled into my old 1930 Chevrolet and drove back up to the cabin and down the long, familiar road to it. I spun to a stop, and sure enough, a young boy about fifteen came running out to us.

"Who are you?" he asked in a rude way.

"Give this letter to Dan Swain. You understand me?" I spoke testily to the brat standing before me. He grabbed the letter and turned around.

"Dad!" he shouted at the top of his lungs. "Letter for ya'!" the boy ran for the cabin while we made our getaway.

The letter read, "Stay away from us. Leave us alone. We have to think about this. Do not come to Ardenville. We will be in touch later. Go ahead and use the cabin."

That's all it said.

Stark reality set in. The Shadow had found us again. We didn't know what to do, so we planned our getaway one step at a time, feeling our way along. All of us retired immediately. Ben and Andy gave notice at their jobs the next day. Like me, they were bachelors in their fifties with enough money saved they could live carefully the rest of their lives. Dan didn't come around.

They didn't know it, but I had more money than they did put together and a permanent income. I could help them out if they ever needed it, so money wouldn't be a problem. While Ben and Andy turned in their notices, I finally sold the huge, silent Victorian house on Main Street. There was people wanting it for a long time anyway. People who wanted to live in a goldfish bowl. Andy and Ben let their rent houses go and we stored the things we wanted to keep in the garage bays. I boarded up the windows and locked the doors to the garage and hired a security company to guard it.

In a little over a month, it was all handled. We were free to leave. I thought it would be hard, but it was easy. We never went back to the cabin. We never heard from Dan again. He knew we didn't want him to come near Ardenville so Map Girl would be protected.

The next step in our plan was to get out of Ardenville. It was time. Better late than never. We wandered around town a few times to see if there was something valuable we might miss before we left. Something that might cause us to want to stay, but there wasn't anything.

During the last month, we refined our plan. We decided to head for Map Girl's place. That's as far as we could plan. It was giant leap, going all that way, but we figured we might as well go as far as we could and see what happened. We were three old guys who'd been shocked out of our little lives by an unexpected intrusion into our private space, the only space we ever owned that we could relax in. Someone else probably might have adjusted to or even welcomed the intrusion, but we couldn't.

The cabin held our fears at bay. We didn't suffer so much when we were there. We owed our Shadows, but not all the time, and not every weekend. We were able to set them aside for days or hours at the cabin. That was over now. Finished. We needed to find a new place; we didn't want to go back to the lonesome, mainly nonstop, fearsome misery we lived in before we bought the cabin to escape to. That meant leaving the town we grew up in. Now we were three old, fear filled gypsies heading out on the road for the first time.

We met in Stoverton. Ben drove his 1951 blue and white Dodge. Andy drove his 1952 station wagon. I was in my old black 1930 Chevy. All three cars were in tip top shape. I kept them that way. We planned to stay a day or two in Stoverton or maybe take right off, whatever worked out for us.

I went into the travel agency and bought us four of the large maps like the one I sold Map Girl so many years ago. They were all new and up to date. The fourth map was for her. The old one she left with was outdated now.

We parked behind a grocery store in an empty parking lot and mapped out our route. There was an underlying urgency about our leaving. Somehow, I knew Map Girl needed us. All of us. When we were ready, we caravanned out of Stoverton, heading for New Mexico, and Map Girl. For better or worse, Bud Spinner, Andrew Noble, and Ben Bass were on the road.

Among angels, there are more than seven hundred words for snow.

Chapter Seven

Mama's Place

These days I spend my time looking through the few pictures I have of Cowboy Johnson, moving from the bed to the table to the rocking chair on light, dry feet that no longer have any sound left in them.

Cowboy Johnson passed away unexpectedly on a hot midsummer day while he was out back by the campfire. There! I said it. Now you know. I can barely say it to myself. I have to catch my breath and rush my words and stop quick and back off after I say it. I put all that together as an answer. It was the best I could do. Lord God.

I don't know what he was doing out there. I only remember seeing him laying in the sand like he was sleeping, his white shirt shining like a flag when I walked out on the back porch. Suddenly, I knew. Hell and arthritis couldn't have held me back from leaping the porch steps and running to him. I turned him over and cradled him close. I talked to him, for I knew before I got there that his soul was surprised at his sudden passing and needed comforting until it found its new bearings.

The years had flown by, and they were good. I looked at his jeans and boots. I smoothed his stick straight hair back and kissed his thoughtful forehead. A long time went by. I sat on the sand and held him and recapitulated his Goodness to the angels in service of him. I told them everything I knew about him. They told me that he'd been filled with a lot more love than hours to spend it.

Timmon found us. I wouldn't let go of him.

"Just let me have a little more time with him. He's not settled over there yet," I begged.

Timmon nodded. He sat down on a log and cried the tears I would never be able to. He sobbed loud and long and keened for this good man we lost in the blink of an eye. I kept watch with my Sight and after a long time, I knew he'd settled into knowing where he was. Many people are disoriented when they first leave this body behind. Like anything new, it takes them awhile to assess the new situation. Some people's spirits scream and cry and try to stay but the inexorable moves them on.

He didn't like it, I could tell, but he was one to accept the inevitable. I watched as the emergency team of angels, guides and beings surrounded him, and quickly worked with his energy. They applauded him, clapping in approval of the good job he'd done here on Earth. They gave him praise.

"You did a good job!" they said. He nodded. They took his hands and pulled him forward. He wanted to look back at me, to have an ending, but he couldn't. He wasn't allowed. Nobody ever is. There was just going forward for him.

I watched the back of him until he disappeared into the distance with them. The others watched me watch him. I knew they were there to stop me from killing myself so I could go with him. I wanted to go after him, but they placed a veil in front of me and sternly ordered me not to cross it.

A long time later, after I was done explaining to him how much he was loved, that we would never forget him, not for one single minute, that we would join him later, it was just a matter of time, I nodded to Timmon. He stood up and walked toward the store, his shoulders slumped. He would call everyone. I stayed where I was, holding the man I would love forever until they came, and I had to let his body go.

*

Land Yachts. Why don't people who drive 1963 Studebaker Avanti's ever pick up hitch hikers? Why do Chrysler Le Baron's never go to where they are needed? And the graceful Plymouths and sturdy Desoto's? Why do they leave it up to the drivers of nondescript pickup trucks, weary vans, and rusty station wagons to transport the weary of limb, the tired of foot and life's many rejected angels toward their mystic destinations?

Maybe hitchhikers dream of riding in a Chrysler, too. I did, and I am a hitchhiker again, right now, waiting again. Got another road to travel. Again. All of us spend time sitting in our own personal "travel agency" while dreaming of holy, beautiful places on this Earth. I found my holy place and tarried here awhile. Now it's time to move on again.

Maybe there are some people spending time living in a negative location in the big empty, like I did before I hit the road with Geena all those years ago. Maybe that's one of the ways we learn where to place ourselves on this planet. Most of us are acutely unconscious of how the universe operates anyway. We make social contracts of avoidance to maintain a known destination. But perhaps that hitchhiker out there is a person who knows something we don't. Perhaps they have a message for us. Or maybe a bottle cap with a star on it.

Some people go further and attempt to gain freedom through madness instead of motion. But that's a hard road to travel, it's a hell of a job, and nobody can maintain regular visits to that part of life locked up behind cell doors. Then there is the clown who knows that healing humor always survives, even in the worst parts of life. But who the hell wants to stay funny all the time except a professional comedian, and they might or might not profit from it. Those are just some of the places in life that some misfits visit here on this planet called Earth. But us, we ended up at Cowboy Johnson's Desert Store. This place saved us. Life made simple. Living in a desert. Not too many takers for the simple kind of Hell we turned into a heaven.

*

William the Dude flew into Albuquerque by himself.

"Algestine said she is getting too old to fly." he said. We were all relieved. Timmon picked him up and brought him straight to the store. We lamented our loss together, holding old hands and stroking old hair. Some of the misfits couldn't get here in time for his cremation. Timmon and Emma were here, and Geena flew in from Carolina. Normaine and Eddy

62

were on some kind of retreat in Canada and we couldn't get in touch with them. The Mafia sisters prayed for him at their church in California. Geena was as heartbroken as we were.

"Cowboy Johnson was a father to me from the instant I met him. I couldn't have asked for a better father. The sound of his name silenced all my demons."

She mourned and walked the desert. She came back from one of her walks and said, "I want the red cactus desert painted fresh and standing up straight again. They will be needed."

William nodded and went to the phone to order paint, wood, containers and new two by fours delivered. Because it was our secret place, he would do the work himself.

Cowboy Johnson was cremated as he asked to be. He'd mentioned a few times that he wanted to go back to being a part of nature when he passed. He believed in reincarnation and cremation. I carried his ashes home to the store. We decided to wait until the Christmas gathering when everybody was home to spread his ashes out on the desert. We stashed his urn beneath his cot for safekeeping. I slept on top of the cot at night to protect him from the Shadows.

We built a campfire every night for a week. We tried eating fried Spam sandwiches and Pepperidge Farm Distressed Chocolate Cake and we roasted marshmallows and bologna on sticks. But nobody's heart or appetite was in it. The first night we drank Pabst Blue Ribbon, the first beer that Cowboy Johnson pushed into my hand when we met. The next night it was Stroh's. Then Black Label,

Michelob, Schlitz, and last of all, Guinness in honor of his ancestors.

William and Timmon went out to the ranch during the day and caught up on ranch stuff. The week flew by. Geena flew home to Carolina. William stayed until I could focus enough on him to understand what needed to be done right away. Cowboy Johnson never left a will.

"He thought there was plenty of time to make one out." William said ruefully. I watched his hands shake. He sat down and bowed his head and stared at the floor. I'd never seen him look so old. He sighed, looked down at his hands and rubbed them together. They made a dry, hopeless sound. He studied me with his sky blue eyes.

"Want me to tell you what I know about him? About the man I called a brother? I'd like to talk about him for a little bit."

"Yes." I breathed, hungry for any connection to our lost one. He sighed and looked down at his open hands. Silence settled around us. When it was deep and tender enough, he poured his waiting words into the soft air.

"I met Avery Mott Judson in California when we were both young men. We both attended schools in Ojai, California. I was sent to board at Villanova Prep for high school, and Avery had been boarding at Ojai Valley Boarding School since he was eleven or so. His brother Perry was older, away at an Ivy league school back east. Our schools were just a mile apart.

Avery's family was and is, very wealthy. So is mine. Our families own strings of houses as well as other things, and one of theirs was in Santa Barbara.

They came to the Santa Barbara house once year on a random weekend to visit with Avery.

Age was not the common denominator in our friendship. Loneliness was. We fell in together and went skiing in the nearby mountains and to the beach. Our parents paid boarding fees for us, but we mostly lived at Avery's parent's big empty place in Santa Barbara. We paid the servants not to report us to our parents. Perry came out to visit as often as he could. Perry and Avery liked each other. They looked alike and thought alike. But unfortunately, the family earmarked Perry for becoming a big shot and making them famous, and so his time with Avery was limited. They saw to it. They ignored Avery in favor Perry.

After I graduated high school, I was packed off to Switzerland for college but I spent my summer vacations in California with Avery. Nobody even knew we were friends. We needed companionship and we were too guarded and distant to make friends with the jolly boys around us. I felt like an exalted mentor to Avery—for a while that is.

Avery's birth mother left him when he was a baby. She was living somewhere in Europe. Avery never knew her. It seemed that she just wasn't interested enough to give a damn about him. There was a big family scandal Avery was involved in when he was ten. It was a pack of lies told by his second stepmother. She had two daughters and a son. One of them drowned their brother and the stepmother blamed it on Avery. His father sent him away and bought the police off saying it was an accidental drowning. That's when he got sent away for good. That's why he was always alone."

He shrugged and glanced at me and then away with watery, light filled blue eyes. I stared at him. Now he too would be filled with a fountain of tears that would never stop running.

"His first stepmother ignored him. His second stepmother hated him. She was poor when she married into the Judson's. It went to her head, and she became arrogant with her words and ways. Avery bore the brunt of it because he is the blood son of his father. Perry chose to avoid it all by staying away from the whole family. I never got to know Perry very well. I know he reads and collects rare books and has a few small vintage sports cars. A 1958 Porsche Three fifty six Speedster, a Shelby Cobra from 1962, a silver 1961 Jaguar E Type, an Aston Martin, a 1957 300 SL Gull Wing Mercedes."

I watched him warm to the subject of old cars. He seemed almost happy for a minute.

"And of course, Perry has always had Corvettes, and a red Alfa Romeo Spider."

I watched as his face grew sad again.

"But I digress," he said apologetically.

"Avery's second stepmother Dawn was never happy. Still isn't. The money wasn't enough. She treated both Avery and his father badly. She wanted someone better to be her spouse. And, she wanted better sons. She harped on it to them all the time.

Dawn was almost beautiful and vicious—mean as a snake. She put Avery's father to work spending money on her, traveling, and keeping his mouth shut. He'd already learned how to do that from his mother.

When we got a little older, Avery and I began to travel together. We went to India and met Krishnamurti. We had no philosophy of life or how it was supposed to be lived, or any purpose. Until we met him, we were just scared boys running away from evil stepmothers and uncaring fathers."

I looked at him questioningly.

"Yes, I had one of those, too."

"Oh."

I thought about this for a minute.

"Who was Krishnamurti? How did he help you and Cowboy… I mean Avery?"

"He was a philosopher and teacher of the divine aspects of life. Without meeting him, I believe that both Avery and I would have eventually destroyed ourselves."

"Oh," I shuddered. I knew about lost souls. I searched desperately for something consoling to say to him, but all I met was my own misery.

"Anyway, we were on a road trip when I bought the ranch. I'd just met Emma's mother and you know about that. My family wasn't interested in me or her. They hoped I would find a debutante, not a lesser person of questionable background to marry. That's all they ever said about it. They didn't attend our wedding and they never said a word when Emma was born. We didn't exist to them. After that time ended, I moved back here to the ranch to get away from family and memories. They made it easy for me to hide from them. They didn't care if Avery and I dropped out of sight. Then Avery bought the church and converted it into a gas station and store, so we could hang out together. We both changed our names to get away from our families and start over."

William shrugged.

"That's it?"

He stood up and brushed off his jeans and dusted his hands with air.

"There's tragedies and stuff, but I've had enough of Memory Lane for now. We'll talk more another time when I can stand it."

He shuffled over to the closet door by Cowboy Johnson's chest of drawers. That damn endless closet! What the hell was in there? He stepped in and came back out with a cardboard box in his hands. He shoved the box under the cot, patted my shoulder, and left. People came with briefcases and went through the box and the closet, where they found more papers. William handled it. A few days later, Timmon drove William back to the airport. The gas station, grocery store and motel were legally mine now. So was a bunch of other stuff, including a lot of money. William had seen to me, and I was grateful to him for it.

*

For now, I still hang the pretty blue flowered apron Cowboy Johnson gave me after everybody moved away on a nail by the kitchen sink and stare out the window above the sink at the flat desert outside. I hope that someday he will meet me back at this desert store when I get ready to die. Maybe I will be back here from my road trip by then. You see, I read his journal, and there are some things that need rectifying, requiring another trip to California. Only, this time, I will stay awhile. Until the job is done. I plan to head out in the spring.

Maybe when the time comes right, when I am back from California, if I make it back, me and Cowboy Johnson will find ourselves dancing together again like we did that night we first met, when our souls danced pinkly in the back room of this store. So young we were back then, when the many ages we'd been met again and embraced each other in a timeless waltz in this little reformed church out in the desert where souls used to meet and shout halleluiah.

I don't know the way for anyone else, and I don't know the answers either. I have always been simple and naïve. At least that's what I've been told. People take it for granted that I don't know much. Maybe thtat's because I'm from the mountains. Mountain folk carry larger Shadows than flatlanders do. We carry the conscience of the ancients forward and out into the world as a reminder to the others we share this world with that there are roots to be dealt with no matter where they are.

We are the keepers of mountain stories. Stories of ghosts, and "hain'ts" and the terrible, raw happenings that keep our people mourning in the cemeteries for twenty years over a single gravestone. Yes, me and mine help carry the larger aspects of the Shadows that have hidden themselves in the shades of the mountains forever.

While I am on my trip, Cowboy Johnson's Desert Oasis will be kept open for any Unexpected Guests and the Known and Unknown Gods that may care to visit this former church. The Hideous Green Sofa awaits them if they need it. That's my plan. Timmon will run the store until I get back, if I ever do.

This is what I know about us Misfits.

We have all survived.

We have all cared about each other.

We are all still in the process of becoming collectors of and connoisseurs of Goodness, for beyond truth, lies an angelic realm called Goodness. Goodness is an active force, just as evil is, only a hell of a lot stronger. Sometimes kindness is wiser than exposing the truth. Other times, without the truth, no kindness or forgiveness can be obtained.

There was a golden age when Normaine and Eddy laughed through passionate days and nights and Geena woke up to proper male love through Cowboy Johnson fathering her and Ray being her sweetheart. I fell in love for the first and last time, and William the Dude and the three Mafia sisters were imported dark wines flowing with hormones.

Maybe the world will someday be healed and reborn with the help of some of our left handed, albeit a little left of center- Goodness. Till' then, we move on. We are all nomads of time. That's when a fine machine like a 1955 Oldsmobile convertible in pale tangerine and orange or a subdued, classy 1958 Chevrolet Impala in forest green with a white leather interior is a godsend.

Here is a history of the store as told by little Celia.

Once upon a time, there was an angel's Kingdom called Goodness. Goodness is always busy doing stuff for other people, like finding lost lizards and helping them by putting them back out in the desert. The people that live here find lost people who come to the store. They give them rides to places in fancy old cars and food to eat and smile at them a lot to help them feel better.

Here is how it started. The Kingdom of Goodness was a church once upon a time in the desert, so there was nobody much around except crosses and singing books and dancing people that fell asleep right in the middle of their dancing 'cause they got all sleepy. Then the church filled up with too much Goodness, and it turned into Cowboy Johnson's Desert Oasis, and all these people had big cars and slept in them so Cowboy Johnson made them a row of rooms with beds to sleep in so their cars wouldn't get rusty.

All the misfits that live at the store love me best. They are my Grandmas, grandpas, aunts, uncles and cousins. But I couldn't use all their love, so they brought in more people to love on when I am not here."

A blizzard is a snowstorm with very strong winds.

Chapter Eight

Bud, Ben and Andy on the Road

We drove the speed limit and never strayed across the center line of the highways. We stayed sedate and cautious. We followed every rule we knew about the big world out there. The big towns scared the hell out of us. But we gritted our teeth and got through each one. Then we stopped on the other side of each one and took a long break before traveling on. We got in and out and walked around and ate snacks and breathed deep some more.

There was no going back.

We learned as we traveled.

It didn't take us long to stop trying to travel as the crow flies. Too many big cities in our way. We got out our maps and laid out a new route each day, depending on what we encountered the day before. Live and learn. We did. Fourteen hundred miles or so, as the crow flies to get to Map Girl's place. We didn't care how long it took us or how far out of the way we needed to go, as long as we avoided all the big cities to make it easier on us. We wanted to travel country roads and take our time. We didn't know what we were going to do when we got to the store anyway. May as well take our time and see what we could find along the way. Nobody back there in

Ardenville ever took on the task of getting to know us. Even if they tried, we probably wouldn't have let them in.

Not being much for talking all of our lives, we learned to apply meanings to things instead. We crawled slowly across the country, always heading south and west. We took turns mapping out the next day's route through small towns. We each added in a little sightseeing here and there to keep our nerves down.

On the days when Ben led the way, we stopped at science museums, lakes, train stations, and barbeque joints. When Andy led, we stopped at car dealers, tractor dealers and gas stations with food for sale. When I led, we stopped at bookstores, art museums, any old place that caught my eye.

We rambled across the country, edgy and full of nerves, waiting for the Dodge, the Ford or the Chevy to quit on us, but they never did. We waited for sandstorms and heat waves and other natural disasters to stop us, but the weather stayed warm and clear and sometimes hot. No police, no tickets, and not too bad food and rooms to stay in each night. The shoe we waited for never dropped.

We were each alone, and yet together on the road. Each day we rode in the privacy of our cars. The Dodge, Chevy and Ford gave us privacy to mutter about life and each other in. At night we stayed in separate motel rooms. We met every night for supper and I told them a little bit more about how me and Map Girl met and what I knew about the life she'd endured back in Ardenville before she successfully ran away. We were changing. We knew it, too. Her story made us grow. Our travels made us grow. Our mission made us grow. Our sedate old masks got chips in them from it. Sometimes we flinched and sometimes we grinned while the dying, worn out Ardenville masks steadily fell away.

We drove through Indiana, Illinois, Missouri, Oklahoma. In Texas, we looped north through the panhandle up into New Mexico. There wasn't much to see on the route we chose. We liked it that way. We were all overwhelmed by natural places like mountains. None of us would ever go near a place like the Grand Canyon or the ocean on purpose. Thank God we weren't born near anything more exciting than a good fishing lake. That was enough of a challenge.

The inspiration that came from mountains or tons of water rushing eternally back and forth on beaches might have been good for others, but not for us. All it did was overwhelm us. We got away as quick as we could.

We were content with sand and two lane roads and the scrub brush we were traveling through. No challenges, no space to not be safe in. Wide open and empty. No people staring and talking. Throughout our lives, we embodied stark fear and emitted distress. In this huge space filled with nothing much, that part of us came to rest. Why bother staying stirred up, when there was nothing around?

One night we took out the map and realized we would arrive at Map Girl's tomorrow. We stopped at a little motel in the afternoon. We needed to plan our entrance. There was no restaurant nearby, just a little store with not much in it, so we ate peanut butter sandwiches, drank milk, and talked about getting to the store the next morning.

"You take the lead, of course," Ben and Andy agreed, staring at me owlishly. I nodded and gulped.

"What time should we get there?" they asked me.

"I don't know," I said.

"Does she sleep in?"

"I don't know."

"Does she get up early?"

"I don't know."

We all three fell silent. After a couple of minutes Andy said, "Let's go about noon. That should work."

"What are you going to wear?" Ben asked me.

I scratched my head.

"I don't know. I never thought about it."

They frowned at me.

"Well, you can't wear your usual get up."

They eyed my sweaty gray tee shirt and dark green work pants with distaste. We all sighed and looked down. Optimistic types were extinct, like dinosaurs, in our experience. We were far from optimistic. How could we convey to Map Girl our good intentions? Put our best foot, or should I say best feet, forward?

We paced in a few circles and around a few imaginary geometric corners, they were engineers, after all, before we all arrived at the same conclusion at about the same time.

Now we knew what to do! We should dress up optimistically for Map Girl. We looked at each other in consternation. Well, we had the answer now, but no solution. Our clothes were nothing to write home about. Our cars were packed full, neatly of course, but we each owned just a small suitcase filled with mostly plain summer clothes in black, dark blue, dark brown and dark greens. Nobody knew what was in each other's luggage, but we'd deduced a few things from being together for the past few weeks.

Andy and Ben had tossed their regulation work clothes, including black Fedora hats, skinny ties and black dress shoes out when they retired. They told me that much. So much for dress clothes.

We'd purchased matching turquoise bowling shirts from "The Pin" bowling alley over in Summit on a dare one afternoon, and we all owned canvas sneakers because of bowling. The sneakers matched our turquoise shirts. We were all about the same height, but I was stockier than either one of them. I studied the two of them. They stared back at me and waited.

"Let's face it, none of us are clothes horses," I finally said morosely.

"Speak for yourself," they both said.

Ben looked like a medium tall, pale, thin, bushy-browed and very hairy twitchy owl hiding behind a pair of thick black glasses. His black hair was very curly and thick and he exuded sweat and mysterious stuff all the time. His hands and feet were small. He was a thinker who shifted from one foot to the other when his nerves were acting up. He looked like he was doing a little dance most of the time. He didn't wear shorts. He said his legs were too skinny. He wore plain black clothes, mostly. Once in a while, I'd seen him in something gray, I don't remember what.

Andy became a frozen, icy chunk of towheaded, thin haired stubbornness when he was scared. He looked like an old Bing Crosby with his sharp chin, pale blue eyes and clear smooth skin that tanned instantly. He was slow to answer because he always needed to think about it first. He didn't mind wearing shorts at all. But they were always down to his knees, and plaid, and in his favorite colors of red or green. That was his Scots ancestry. Took the place of a kilt, he said. Andy's hands and feet were large. He looked calm and capable. When he did talk, people listened. It was Andy who got Ben hired on at the factory.

I stared at them, waiting, but no answer to this dressing up problem approached me in any way.

"Back in fourth grade, Leah Firth told me I had caramel colored eyebrows," Andy finally offered. "I like that color."

Ben nodded.

"They called me Goth Boy in junior high because I like to wear black."

None of that changed the fact that we didn't have the clothes we needed to meet Map Girl in. Map Girl was the psychic Queen of the Road. The Destinator of us all. I admit, I may have embellished the story of Map Girl a little more each time we shared dinner on the road getting here. But only by a sentence or two each time. Besides, we needed to have a destination and a reason for it, and Map Girl was it.

After a long silence, I stated my sad conclusion.

"We managed all of our lives to not let the judgmental attitudes of a whole town overcome us by not drawing attention to ourselves, and it has left us the owners of drab, uninspiring, skimpy wardrobes."

Then determination set in.

"But we're not back there anymore. And I don't plan on ever going back. We've come this far to get away from hiding out, so maybe we could learn to wear something different now and be seen. We passed a western clothing store not far back, remember? Maybe we could find something there."

"No."

Andy and Ben shook their heads in unison.

"Picking out clothes is kind of like picking out cars. Besides it's the only store for miles around, " I wheedled.

"I mean, this is sort of out west, so we may as well look the part and fit in. We can't let Dan Swain overcome us when a whole town couldn't. Remember his Hawaiian shirts and those awful green shorts he wore with all the baggy pockets in them? We can do better than that."

We strolled cautiously into the western store. Andy headed for a caramel colored cowboy hat with a dark brown band around it perched on a peg just inside the door. Ben headed for a row of black western shirts. He chose a shirt made of rayon gabardine with a label from a fancy ranch in California. A rainbow was embroidered on the front, and the collar had striped piping. The half moon pockets looked like outhouse windows with rainbow embroidered darts. It had pearl snaps and gauntlet cuffs.

"Yep. It is like buying a car."

He scowled at me.

"You should have told us that sooner."

He wandered off to buy more clothes.

Andy chose a silk twill western shirt in cantaloupe with a long dart collar sporting hideaway loops, gathered seams and pleats down the front to go with his caramel colored cowboy hat.

I picked out a Dumont Original Argyle western shirt with a square hem in light blue. It had a silver and blue sparkly cactus embroidered on the front. I found a pair of black pants and a lightweight, straw colored cowboy hat to go with it.

Andy picked out new jeans, caramel colored moccasins, a couple of lemon yellow bandanas, and a turquoise western tie. Not to be outdone, Ben chose a black felt cowboy hat with a band of small silver conchos, a matching bracelet, and black gabardine pants to go with his new shirt.

We looked at the cowboy boots, but our feet hurt just thinking about them. Ben and I would wear our loafers and Andy would wear his sneakers.

Yep. We were learning to see past our old understanding. It was time for it to expire. Now Map Girl would see that we were well dressed, up to date guys, not antiquities from another era. Loaded with new shirts, pants and extras, including a cowboy deodorant, we drove back to the motel. The next morning we dressed up and got on the road. Sagebrush and sand and cactus were all that claimed our attention until we sighted the store.

I stayed in the lead because I knew Map Girl. I was deadly scared. Maybe there was a deeper mission at work here. But if there was, I sure as hell didn't know what it was. Did Map Girl remember me? What if she didn't? Or what if she didn't give a damn? I drove past the store to give myself time to think it out. Andy and Ben followed me like ducks following their mother. I thought some more. I turned around and drove past the store going the other way. They followed me. I turned and drove past again with Ben and Andy following me.

Eventually, I worked out Plan B. If she didn't like us, we would move on to California. That was the place everybody in Ardenville aspired to visit at least once. They came back changed. More respected, almost revered even though some of them were idiots and mean. I drove back and forth past the store six times before I got up enough courage to pull in. I pulled over to the side of the store and stopped beside a dusty green El Camino.

Ben and Andy pulled in and parked beside of me in a neat row. I deep breathed and looked over at Andy and Ben. All of my self-worth and every other damn thing was right up in my face, challenging me every which way about this.

Andy and Ben were poring over their road maps, deliberately not looking at me. I got the message. They were indicating that if this didn't work out, then we would just travel on. They knew about shyness. There were more places in the world than this and we could go to one of them. I immediately felt better. I took Map Girl's new map out of the glove box and stepped out of my 31' Chevy. Ben and Andy stepped out of their cars and shut their doors and waited. I took the lead again.

I was wearing my new ice blue western shirt with the sparkly cactus on it, new black jeans, a straw colored cowboy hat, and my tan loafers. I had a blue plaid bandana tied around my neck. Ben wore his black rayon shirt with the rainbows embroidered on it, black jeans, and the black cowboy hat with the silver ring of conchos around it. He wore a black bandana tied around his neck. He wore his old sneakers, but at least he was clean shaven. Andy was all dolled up. He was cantaloupe and caramel rayon from the top of his cowboy hat down to his tan loafers. Around his neck was a bright yellow bandana.

A canary yellow 1946 GMC Half Ton truck pulled in just as we reached the porch steps. I turned and waited as the older man got out of the yellow truck. He slowed his steps as he got near us. He stopped when he got close, and let out a low, almost reverent whistle. His light blue eyes widened.

"Where you guys from?" he asked in a soft, low voice.

I shrugged and answered for us.

"Everywhere. Anywhere. Nowhere."

"I bet," the man said.

We waited while he looked us over. I didn't know what he thought he might see. We were just three old men on the road. Dressed up fancy.

"You going in the store?" he asked.

"We thought we would," I answered.

"I'll follow you. I always have anyway. My name is William."

The man was talking nonsense.

"We are looking for Map Girl."

He stared at us in surprise. After a minute he said, "Would you mind waiting on the porch for a minute before you go in?"

We nodded nervously and followed him up the steps to wait. He went in the store and came back out carrying three caps with logos on them.

"Would you mind wearing these instead of cowboy hats? She hates cowboy hats. They will set her off, and she don't need that right now."

We took off our new cowboy hats, placed them on the porch chairs, and put the caps on. They were black with beer logos on them. I got a Guinness, Ben got a Pabst Blue Ribbon, and Andy got a Budweiser cap.

We filed into the store with William trailing us. The store was long and narrow. Map Girl stood at the other end of the long room. I'd know her anywhere. She was taping a cardboard box shut. The box was sitting on the long counter. She looked tired and old and discouraged. Gray was in her hair.

Tears filled my eyes. My heart turned over with something I didn't have words for. I stopped and held the new map out to her.

She didn't look up until William said, "Got some people here that have come a long ways to see you."

Map Girl looked up then. She studied us. She blanched, then flushed with high color. She let go of the cardboard box she was holding on to and ran toward us. I backed up and stumbled against Ben and Andy.

The guy named William stepped in front of us and caught her in his arms. Somehow he knew we would have run from her before letting her hug us. Or hug me. He turned her slowly around to us, and said to her, "Do you know these nice men?"

Map Girl nodded. With wonder on her face, she took a step toward me. William held on to her arm.

"Bud? Bud Spinner?"

I nodded in relief. At least she knew me. She looked at my outstretched hand.

"You brought me a new map?"

I nodded.

After a long moment, she said, "How did you know?"

She looked from me to the map I held in my hand and burst out crying.

"I'm going to California!"

William led her to me. I patted her head and face and then Ben and Andy patted her arms and soothed her hands. They moved around to the front of her until we had her surrounded. I don't know how that happened. Then we turned our backs to her and crowded up against her to keep her standing. She rubbed the backs of our heads and leaned on us and held our shoulders and kneaded them with grief filled, angry hands as she told us about Cowboy Johnson.

"He's dead! He was my man, my good man, and now he's gone! I hate God!" she wailed.

She blubbered and cried and got the backs of us all wet with tears and snot. We waited it out. Somehow we knew what to do. I guess we just offered what was available. Map Girl was a wounded angel, and we all knew it. An angel who would never understand algebra. A naïve, lovely soul that couldn't count past a dollar bill. I remembered the money I slipped into her purse so long ago, knowing that she needed help from humans as well as angels.

"Where's Geena?" I asked, breaking the spell. I wanted to get her mind off of her grief.

"What is her baby's name?"

Map Girl sighed and hiccupped. She gave us a few more pats and shrugged her way out of our circle. William held her. Waves of like rushed from the three of us toward William and Map Girl. They stood there and reveled in it for some reason. We looked at each other and shrugged. We didn't like people very often, so maybe we had a buildup of energy going on. The new map fell on the floor when she rushed us. I picked it up and turned sideways and held it out to her. Andy and Ben turned sideways, too.

William laughed.

"It's about time you guys showed up! You three look like a Doo Wop backup group for a fifties band. What a disguise! Let's go in the back room."

I wondered what the hell he was talking about.

We followed them towards the back of the store and stepped cautiously inside the glass partition and looked around. It was big. There was a table, a cot, a kitchen and a back door. And the ugliest green sofa I have ever seen.

William led Map Girl over to the ugly green sofa where she nestled into a corner of it. He handed her a blue paisley shawl and grinned at us.

"The Hideous Green Sofa," he explained, pointing to the ugly sofa Map Girl was sitting on. Ben and Andy nudged me. I needed to complete my mission. I edged over to Map Girl and tossed the new map on her lap. She took it in her hands, shook it open and hollered, "I'm going to California!" again and burst into tears.

Andy, Ben, and I looked at each other, trying to figure out what to do next. It was time to run. None of us could take any more. William interrupted our desperate thoughts. Somehow he knew we were teetering on the edge.

"I need some help over here," he said.

"Let's get the spaghetti made. We'll need a ton of it. That's what she needs when she gets like this," he explained. We blanched. Who was he going to feed? An army? Yes, we had changed. We could handle more. But we did not want more company than was already here. William noted our reaction.

"It's just us. Us two and my daughter Emma. She's an artist. You may know of her. Emma Makepeace?"

We nodded. Of course we knew of her. We eyeballed each other. She was world famous. Sure she was his daughter. He was just kidding us about her being his daughter.

We set to work, learning how to make tons of spaghetti without many words but with plenty of sauce while Map Girl alternated between wailing and napping on the Hideous Green Sofa. That sofa held a long history, according to William. Evidently, it carried the burdens and sorrows and happiness of many an occupant. Making spaghetti for its occupants was a long history too.

We had changed. We were dressed up, spaghetti making roadies now. Eating in strange restaurants each night. Sleeping in strange beds in strange rooms. If we could do that, we could be here for a dinner with Emma Makepeace, just in case what the old geezer claimed was true. We were definitely dressed for it in our western shirts with pearl snap cuffs, just in case William wasn't kidding. We'd put on cowboy deodorant earlier, too.

How the hell could this happen? Emma Makepeace was one of the most spiritual artists on the planet. I owned posters of her work. Ben and Andy went to museums to admire her art. Gifts. That's what today was all about. Maybe not later. But today. We were all getting and giving gifts. When the spaghetti was done, we turned in a few slow circles, taking in this place and this new situation. We were learning to integrate even more. This place felt good. Almost holy.

William watched us and said, "This gas station and store used to be a church. For over a hundred years."

He waited while we turned in a few more slow circles.

Then he said, "Follow me, boys."

He led us out to the back porch. We filed out the back door behind him. Barbeque grills of all sizes and kinds were lined up neatly on the wide, long, porch, like horses about to have a race. He went back inside and came back out with four Pabst Blue Ribbons in his hands and handed them around. He wiped the sweat from his forehead.

"Spaghetti making is hard work when it's hot out. Good thing God ...I mean somebody, invented beer."

We stared at him. He was treating us like we were choirboys again. What the hell? We shrugged and sipped our beers and looked around. Far be it from us to say anything. We had never been admired before for anything and it felt good. Maybe he was just dazzled by our new clothes.

87

Winds blowing in from the north makes snow stick to the south side of trees.

Chapter Nine

The desert. We were in it. And it wasn't so bad. But...

"Are there any scorpions or bugs close by?"

I tried to ask my question casually. Andy and Ben tensed up, waiting for the answer.

"Nah. We haven't seen any scorpions around here in a long time. You have to go looking for bugs if you want to find them. Too close to the road. Too much traffic and too many people these days." William said.

We glanced at each other, relieved.

"How about we fire up a couple of grills and slap some steaks and burgers on them for dinner? Maybe a few veggies and a couple taters too?"

We set to work. William brought us more beer and left. Ben examined his spatula and said, "This is kind of like cooking on the deck back at the cabin."

Andy said, "Yeah. Only in a desert."

I said, "Yeah. Don't forget the beer."

William came back out and handed each of us a key.

"You'll need rooms. Room Four. Room Five. Room Six."

He pointed at the long, low blue motel on the other side of the dusty parking behind the back porch.

"Thanks," we said.

We finished grilling and carried the food in. Then we fled to our motel rooms to get as swanky as we could before possibly meeting Emma Makepeace. After we were ready, we went and stood on the back porch.

William came out and took one look at our red faces and outfits and went back inside. He was still wearing the faded blue jeans and old blue shirt he was wearing when we met him. Ben still wore his same outfit, but he'd added a belt that sparkled and glittered like diamonds. Andy changed his shirt to one of lemon and lime colored cactus on a tan background. I stayed the same. Still in blue. Still froze in place, as usual.

William came back out in a minute with more bottles of beer in his hands. Stroh's longnecks. Cold and icy. We needed them.

I expected to be more nervous than I was. Meeting Emma Makepeace would be like meeting a movie star. We'd been awed by her work for years. Her paintings glowed with light and color and an enduring spiritual reality.

We waited in rockers on the back porch until she got to the store. William said Map Girl was taking a nap. She would eat a little something later. We heard a car pull in. William went inside. In a few minutes, he called us in to eat.

Emma Makepeace was already seated at the table. She was holding a glass of water in one hand and a napkin in the other. We knew it was her from her pictures. We almost threw ourselves on the floor in gratitude for not having to hug her or to even shake her hand. We worshipped her, all right. From afar.

She smiled at us from the ocean of calm she sat in. She was small and slim and brown haired and dark eyed. She wore her hair in a smooth bun at the nape of her neck. Quiet. Soothing. She wore pearls with her black pants and shirt. I searched for the right word. She had Equanimity.

Before I thought, I spoke.

"Miz Makepeace, how did you get your Equanimity?"

I blushed in horror at what I asked, but she didn't seem to think my question was amiss. I was regretting reading too many of those metaphysical books. She pondered her answer as though the question wasn't unusual.

"I need to think about it. Let me answer that question later. And please, call me Emma."

She turned to William.

"I can tell you that wherever it came from, it was Father that helped me keep it."

They exchanged fond looks and chatted back and forth as they passed the steaks and spaghetti around. William set fresh, frosty beers by our plates. We stayed speechless and sighed for the sweetness of it.

In a few minutes, Miss Emma stood up and said she needed to leave. That there was a couple of things she needed to take care of. As one, we stared down at our plates. We'd failed. We hadn't been witty or charming to this lovely woman. We hadn't asked her any questions. We hadn't made small talk. We stared down at our plates, mute in our shame.

"Will you come out to the ranch tomorrow and visit me? Father and I would like to show you around."

We stared at her and then nodded. We had been forgiven.

"Father, can I have a steak and a burger to take home? I'm still a bit hungry, and they are delicious tonight. Good cooks on the grill."

She smiled at us.

William walked her out front and stayed awhile. We turned back to our dinners and hastily cleaned our plates and drank our beers. William strolled back in. We were embarrassed, but William just looked around and said morosely.

"I guess it's time to do the damn...I mean darn...dishes. Anybody want to help?"

He looked at us hopefully. I snickered while Ben coughed behind his hand and Andy fanned his hands out and stared at them with a grin. We were changing. We'd just spontaneously proven it to each other.

How did Emma Makepeace known when we were just at the breaking point, another one, ready to jump up from the table and run? I shuddered. Thank God she never used the word "love" when she invited us out to the ranch. "Like" was a hell of a lot easier to deal with.

Some things never change, and that was all right. No matter how much we changed, we would always avoid the "L" word.

How did William known to stay away until we finished eating? Maybe they understood a little bit of how we were? Whatever the reason, at least they were kind. After the clean-up was done, me and Ben and Andy headed for our motel rooms. William stopped us.

"Want to set on the back porch just a couple minutes?"

"No."

"No"

"No."

The verdict was unanimous.

William blinked.

"I just want to know how you met Map Girl."

We sighed and looked at each other. It was okay. We were used to sharing pieces of her story with each other every night in strange restaurants. We could do this. Not for long, though. We headed for the back porch and settled into rockers. William, Ben, and Andy looked at me and waited. I guess I was supposed to be the storyteller. Well, this could get complicated. I decided to make it short. It was anyway.

"Map Girl grew up in the same town the three of us grew up in. It was a mean little place, still is. Probably always will be. Map Girl used to stop at the garage and gas station I own to look over the map I keep tacked up on the office wall. She was always unhappy, so I told her she might get to leave there someday."

I shrugged.

"Just trying to give her hope. I sold her the map she used to get out of town. I knew she was leaving. The last I saw of her until today was her and her daughter pulling out from my garage. Her daughter was twelve."

I didn't mention the money I'd crammed in her purse that Geena put in her pocket. I was still glad of that.

"How long ago was that?"

"She never told you any of it?"

"Nope. You know, some angels don't understand about life. They don't understand about geography or money or meanness. Or maybe I didn't want to know how she got hurt, so I didn't ask," William said.

I studied on his words. So he knew Map Girl was an angel.

"It's a few years past a decade now," I said.

"So you come all this way to bring her a new map after all that time?"

All three of us nodded yes.

"How did you know she needed one?"

"We didn't. It just came time for us to leave that place, so I got us maps like the one she left with, only updated for each of us. So, I got her a new map too, just in case she needed it."

"Where you headed from here?"

Ben, Andy and me looked at each other.

"Don't know," Ben said.

"Maybe California," I said. "We haven't figured that one out yet. We were just glad to get this far."

"Driving through big cities is something I don't like either," William said.

It went dark while we talked. The night lights came on over at the motel. Time for us to go to our rooms. We stood up. We'd had enough for today.

"See you in the morning," William said.

William drove us out to the ranch early the next morning. We were already up and sitting in the rockers on our motel porches when he came to pick us up. Map Girl wasn't around. We dressed up again. After all, it wasn't every day we got invited to visit Emma Makepeace at her ranch.

I wore my new pale lemon yellow short sleeved western shirt with green vines embroidered on the front of it. It was made of a lightweight cotton blend guaranteeing coolness. Andy wore his new butterscotch colored, short sleeved western shirt with the purple leaf pattern embroidered on the front. Ben wore his new short sleeved, black western shirt with the silver outlines of horses running across it.

We climbed in the back of William's canary yellow truck. To his credit, William never batted an eye when we climbed in the back instead of riding in the front with him. Maybe he guessed this was one of our ways of handling too much closeness. We didn't offer to explain it, either.

A short time later, William turned off the highway and onto a dusty lane. We passed under a metal sign over our heads that read "Makepeace Ranch." A few miles further on, William stopped at the house. He got out and shut his door and ambled toward a corral off in the distance. We waited, but he didn't come back. So we climbed out and stood there. Then a Spanish maid carrying a big tray walked past us.

"Follow me," she ordered in a heavy accent.

She led us to a picnic table setting under a couple of big shade trees. On her tray was our breakfast. Big clay mugs of hot soup, scrambled egg tacos, and iced lemonade. We looked at each other.

"Well, at least we'll know where our gas is going to be coming from for the next day," Andy said. We snickered in approval. Another one of us had come up with a joke. We were progressing.

In a while the maid and Emma came out and got us. We helped the maid carry the tray and stuff back to the kitchen. Then we followed Emma through the ranch house. I'd never seen anything like it.

"Frank Lloyd Wright," Andy whispered in awe.

"No. It's a 1951 Hudson," Ben whispered.

"No. It's a 1934 Pierce Arrow," I whispered.

"No. It's a 1938 Auburn 851 Cabriolet," Andy whispered.

"No. It's a silver Rolls Royce, after all."

The three of us accepted this final say. What was, was. By this time, we'd reached the front of the house. We stepped into the living room.

"Oh my God," we whispered and clutched each other. This was like seeing a mountain or the Grand Canyon. Overwhelming. One of those awe filled places we had trouble being in. This was the inside of a house? We looked at each other in consternation and surprise.

Emma said, "I'll be back in a few minutes." She turned and left. We had never seen anything like it in any of the art museums or other places we'd seen. High and holy rivers of colors and shapes wove themselves around us like the robes priests wore in the days of old. Rich and colorful and unapologetic, moving through life with pomp and dignity.

We crowded into a corner of the room and swayed together until we could stand it a little better. Then we were able to move apart and gaze in awe. Then we turned in slow circles for a while and stopped when Emma walked in with William.

"Ready to see more of the ranch? Want to go outside for awhile?"

We nodded vigorously with relief. He understood how we felt. They took us all over the ranch. We looked at barns and stables and corrals and all kinds of animals. We drank more mugs of thin, hot broth and ate sandwiches and drank more lemonade for lunch. Laced with all this, were questions from Emma about us.

After the basic questions about us were answered, like age, make and serial number, which we stayed mute to, her questions turned to our philosophies on life. What did we believe in? Where would we like to live now? Did we like peace and quiet? Did big cities bother us with their noise and bustle? What did we read? Did we like people? Did we have children? Were we ever married? Would we ever like to get married? Did we like the mountains? Did we like the beach? The country? Did we garden? Were we interested in libraries or scheduled lives? We shuddered and quaked and sidestepped our way through all of her awful questions.

She stopped her questions just short of us getting ready to run screaming down the road to get away from them.

"I'm sorry," Emma said in response to the looks on our faces. "I got carried away. We are so excited that you are here with us. And Map Girl, as you call her, is in so much grief from losing Avery that she isn't quite well just now."

"We just don't know how she will be with you, and frankly, we don't want you to leave. We want you to take a sort of long road trip with us. To a place you might like...to stay at for awhile... or visit?"

Uh. Oh. We were in trouble. These people were making plans for us. They sounded like locking up kind of plans. We looked at each other. Evidently, they didn't like our new clothes.

I announced in a strong voice, "We are going back to see Map Girl. Do you want to drive us back? If not, we can walk. But we are leaving right now."

William drove us back to the store. Map Girl was inside, busy pickling eggs in beet juice, sugar, and vinegar in a big glass jar. She smiled the biggest, loveliest smile at us. The best one anyone sent my way since she left Ardenville. I relaxed and my fears ebbed away. Ben and Andy sighed in relief.

"Do you like pickled eggs? I'm making plenty," she said importantly. "They are for the weekend campfire. They will be pickled by then," she explained.

We are here to laugh at the odds and live our lives so sweet that death trembles and runs away when it comes near us. That's what I thought about the angel standing in front of us, who was pickling eggs for a campfire, an angel who just revived us and saved us from our fears with her lovely smile. There would be plenty of trembling done before she ever went her way.

William saved us from having to answer her. The front screen door opened, and he came in carrying a rachet.

"Any of you fellers know anything about 1955 DeSoto Fire Domes? I can't seem to fix the damn...oops! Sorry. I can't seem to fix the darn thing."

We followed him out to the garage and set to work. Andy made a list and Ben went inside and called the car parts place. It was going to be a piece of work, but it could be done. It was a relief to work on the DeSoto. It felt familiar. We ate spaghetti again for supper before we went to our motel rooms. Map Girl was sad and didn't say much, but she stuck close to us. She seemed to know now not to try to hug us or anything like that.

William left after we agreed to let to him pick us up for breakfast out at the ranch. He said someone named Timmon would be back from California in a few days to help Map Girl with the store.

We were to the point we didn't give a damn who came or went. We didn't want to meet anybody else. We just wanted to get the hell out of there. Back to something familiar. But back to where? We couldn't go sightseeing. It was too hard on us. We could die from shock if we saw something like the Rocky Mountains or the ocean, which we had never seen. We didn't want to see any tourist attractions. I guess we would have to head out to California after all.

During a whiteout, visibility and contrasts are severely reduced by snow or sand.

Chapter Ten

I already knew the answer. So did Andy and Ben. We went back to our motel rooms after doing the dishes. We gathered in Ben's room to have a private talk. We still hadn't talked to Map Girl much. Maybe we didn't need to. She seemed to be in a different world than we were. She was friendly, but she didn't seem to be interested in us at all. Maybe we'd come here for nothing.

Ben didn't turn on the lights. We sat on the side of the beds in the dusky light.

"It's time to go back."

Ben and Andy looked at each other mournfully. Andy started scratching.

"Yeah. I'm beginning to break out in hives."

"Yeah. My nerves are shot." Ben held out his hands. They were shaking.

"I feel like a pressure cooker with no outlet," Andy added.

"Me, too," I added. "I think this was a dead end."

We looked at each other sadly. We knew when we started out being runaways we would probably have to go back home. Back to Ardenville. Back to our own personal version of Hell. That's why we were so careful to leave with everybody in town believing that we were just going on a long vacation. Just covering our bases in case the gossips in town wanted to get something started. It is amazing how dull people all of a sudden develop a big imagination when it comes to other people's business.

"You're right. None of us can take much more," Andy said. "It's time to make new plans. Return plans. The Return to Hell plans."

"At least going back, we know the route," Ben added.

"Yeah, that will help us some," Andy said.

"Back to the old one two, I guess."

They sighed.

They were right, so I didn't say a word about going to California. Yep. We had lost. We were three old guys who couldn't stand being out in the world. It was too fast, too noisy, too big, too close, and too unkind for us to handle. We needed a familiar, quiet, peaceful routine if we were to live to be any older. Even if it was an old, mean, routine we'd grown to despise.

"When should we leave?" I asked.

"I can stand a couple more days, that's all," Andy said.

Ben nodded. They would live with the stress a couple more days because of me and Map Girl. Maybe Emma Makepeace would be around. I hoped so.

"I don't want to leave on the weekend. Too much traffic and people and kids on the roads."

"Well, this is Thursday. Monday's four days from now. I don't know if we can stand it that long, but let's give it a try."

"Okay. We'll leave Monday morning, if we don't leave quicker."

We parted ways and went to our rooms. I sat in the silence and thought about my mother for the first time in years. I couldn't pinpoint the last time I thought about her. Maybe I'd got my runaway genes from her.

We were in the garage working on the DeSoto when William came to pick us up early the next morning. We climbed into the back of his canary yellow truck, and off he went. He took his time. The desert was pretty in an odd sort of way early in the morning. Purples shaded through lemon yellows into pale greens across the desert floor as the sun crept steadily up the horizon. We saw a road runner.

Miss Emma was waiting for us. We couldn't call her just Emma. It was more respectful to call her Miss Emma. We said it that way, and she didn't object. Breakfast was served out at the picnic table again. Egg and meat burritos, fried potatoes, fresh tomatoes, sautéed red bell peppers, and hot, creamy mugs of a different soup again. When we were almost done, Miss Emma said to me, "Remember when you asked me where I got my Equanimity?"

I nodded.

"Well, I can tell you that I have learned that Equanimity is an odd thing. A person can gain it and then lose it. It's a way of being that won't stay unless it is supported by something or someone else, maybe a religion or Nature."

She smiled at William.

"The people aware of these things tell me I was born with Equanimity. I needed it because I lost my mother so young. And my father, though the path of Equanimity isn't his, he doesn't need it, has done everything to make sure I can keep it. It's because of him that I am able to keep it. There are places that ensure Equanimity for those of us who are sensitive to the hells this big world around us carry. The Earth is a living Being, and has provided places for those kinds of angels, meaning us too. We just have to find those places."

We listened intently. We'd never been called angels before. Other things. Many of them sometimes. But never angels.

"What places ensure Equanimity, you might ask?" she said, asking the question for us.

"Father and I found a place for people like us up in Oregon years ago, and we go up there and stay for a bit every now and then, until we are refreshed and ready to come back out again."

We understood the need she was talking about.

"What kind of place?" Ben asked.

"It's a private monastery. A different kind of monastery. If you are accepted, you can visit whenever you want, and stay as long as you want. And leave when you want. It's quiet. And peaceful. Monks live there and take care of the place. They grow gardens and do other things."

"We don't care much about religious places," I said.

Miss Emma nodded.

"That's the thing. There is a sanctuary, but only the monks have to attend the services. The people staying there on retreat do not have to go. And, it's not that far away from here. We are ready to head out whenever you are. You have to know certain people to get in, and we do. Think of it as another road trip. You're already on one. May as well visit a place created for people like you. And me. And father."

Miss Emma smiled at us and waited. A blinding smile like Map Girl gave us yesterday. I could see the hope and anxiety in her. She wanted us to go. Badly. Why?

"You're not trying to trap us into living in a disguised mental hospital, are you?"

"No."

She didn't laugh at me.

"You're not trying to take us someplace and get us locked up?"

"Never. You're probably saner than I am."

I remembered her paintings.

"Maybe," I said.

Miss Emma laughed.

"I wouldn't be so pushy, except I think you are going to take off soon and go back to the place you left behind, and I wanted you to look at better choices. You're wrong for that place you left behind, so why not go forward instead? I apologize for talking so much. It isn't like me at all. I don't know why I am so invested in you three wise men, but I promise to go back to being quiet when we get on the road. I just need my Equanimity back like Map Girl needed her new map. I need an Equanimity upgrade. And my father, maybe you have a gift for him too."

She stood up and walked away.

William said, "Should you stay or go? I never know which one to do myself, so I can't answer for you. I sure as hell wish that Avery hadn't died on us.

He knew how to handle this kind of shi... I mean, stuff."

"We have to think about it awhile anyway," I said.

"Are there any big cities in the way of getting there?" Andy asked.

"Nope. None," William answered.

"It's not close to a big city is it?" Ben asked.

"Nope. It's way out in the country."

"Is it as big place? Lots of people?"

"Yup and nope. There is a lot of land and a few buildings. A lake and regular trees and a forest and vegetable gardens. Very few people are ever there. Just a few monks and a few others like us. And they know how to behave. Nobody in your face. Cabins on the lake. Yep. I looked 'em over, but never used one. Not much of a fisherman myself."

We stared at each other. Another cabin on a lake. Just maybe we'd been given another chance.

"Any women or kids go there?"

"Once in a great while a woman will go on retreat there. She usually sits around out of sight and meditates and stuff. No kids allowed. Never have been. The monks are men, not women. Thank God. Women are too gabby."

He pulled a handkerchief from his hip pocket and wiped sweat off of his forehead and volunteered some information we knew nothing about.

"My wife Algestine? Back in California? She never stops trying to run my show. That's partly 'cause she's Italian Mafia with two sisters just like her and why I'm here. At the store. And at the ranch. I needed a break. And I was needed here. .....You can fish all you want to up there boys if you like that sort of stuff."

"Can we have beer at the cabin?"

"They got a small brewery on the property, guys. Every monk works at it, and everybody drinks the beer. A bunch of jolly monks living there!"

He grinned.

"Whew!"

"Is that about it? Know enough to go on another road trip now?"

I asked the question we needed to know about the most.

"Does it snow there?"

"Yes, it does. You get a few feet of snow on the ground for at least five, six months during winter."

He looked at us apologetically.

"It snows to beat hell... I mean, a lot... in the winter."

"We just want you to visit and look the place over. You don't have to stay. You're grownups. Can't nobody make you do stuff now. You're too old. It's just a road trip."

We looked at each other, weighing it out. Grownups. Three Old grownups. Or Groanups. The snow and a cabin and a lake again. That did it for us. But there was one more thing. We looked at William and waited. It took a couple of minutes for him to figure it out.

"Unfortunately, Emma might have other commitments, or she would make the trip with us?"

"Is that it?"

"Part of it. We caravan. Each in our own cars. For privacy. How many miles? How many days?"

"Well, it's close to fifteen hundred miles or so from here."

"We keep to the speed limits, and don't like to get in a big hurry," Andy said.

Ben and me nodded.

"Sometimes we stop to see stuff. Stuff that other people might not be interested in."

Williams eyes brightened with curiosity.

"What stuff? I mean, I might be interested, too. "

"Well. Just this and that," I hedged.

"Maybe a train station or two," Andy said.

"Or we stop to eat ribs or stock up on cheezie puffs," Blabbermouth Ben said. "At night we all get separate motel rooms. But we eat supper together and lay the next day's travel plans out on our maps."

"I leave it in your capable hands," William said, touching his hand to the brim of his hat.

"You ready to go back to the store?"

"Okay, then."

We looked at each other.

"We'll be ready to go in the morning."

A ground blizzard is the lifting and blowing of loose snow or ice on the ground by strong winds.

So are generations

Chapter Eleven

We piled into the back of William's truck and he drove us back to the store. We would be leaving the next morning. Miss Emma waved goodbye, a handkerchief in her hand, tears streaming down her face. We stared at her until we were almost out sight before we remembered to wave back. Somberly we stared at each other. We liked her. She understood us or seemed to. Maybe we would never see her again. Why she was crying? Nobody had ever cried over any of us before. I shuddered. "I'm damn glad I never had a girlfriend!" I muttered. Andy and Ben nodded in agreement.

"Why, this bunch treats us with something close to reverence, like we know something they don't. Us, the three wise men? Or maybe they know something we don't. Boys, we better change back to our old clothes quick if this is what happens when we dress up!"

Ben and Andy nodded. Acceptance. What a strange thing it was. Life wasn't fair, never was. But at least now it was getting more interesting. We were becoming disarmed, and possibly too charming. Relief from the deadly serious gravity we usually carried was causing us to take risks. Would that make us more attractive to the human race?

Fat chance.

What I did know was that all of us were old friends, keepers and protectors of each other's past Lives. The Eastern books I read called it that. All of us. Ben, Andy, William, Map Girl, and Miss Emma, me. Maybe more would show up. Map Girl once said we needed to be misfits to fit in with her little desert store family. We weren't sure what she meant, but we knew we qualified grandly for being Misfits.

*

The guy named Timmon got to the store while we were having a last supper with Map Girl. Spaghetti again. Map Girl didn't say much when we told her we were leaving in the morning with William. "Ah," she said. "William! You'll be fine."

She seemed preoccupied. Then a beautiful young man came in. He was filled with Light and Good. He was tall, blond, tan, and blue eyed. I could tell he had once been around evil; he carried the scars Goodness carries when it has been wounded and healed. Map Girl jumped up and hugged him and introduced him to us.

Timmon smiled and sat down and filled his plate with spaghetti. He didn't seem surprised at the spaghetti or Map Girl's wandering words. We ate in silence while Map Girl rambled on about this and that, whatever crossed her mind. Slowly it dawned on me that Map Girl might not be able to take care of herself. I would have to stay here if she couldn't. I waved my hand at Timmon. He looked at me. I, who never asked questions, gave him a round third degree.

"You staying here?"

"You going to live here and run the store?"

"You, ah... taking care of everything here?"

Timmon quit eating and stared at me. The boy was a little slow on the uptake.

"Map Girl kin to you?"

"You staying put?"

"Here?"

He watched me and finally caught on.

"Oh, yes!"

Map Girl ignored us. Her mind was still elsewhere. I looked at her and back at Timmon. Back and forth.

"You got it handled?"

"Oh yes!" he hastily replied.

At last he volunteered more information.

"It's been all set up for awhile now, ever since..." he glanced at Map Girl and then away.

"William did it. We all help... ah... each other here at the store. None of us is ever left alone here. Mostly. I'm here most of the time now. Or Hector and Annie. They run the place."

He nodded and filled his mouth with spaghetti. I gave him a long look. He was acting a bit like us three. Bashful and not wordy at all.

Map Girl looked at Timmon.

"I'm glad you're home."

"Me too," he answered simply in a voice filled with caring. The love and joy in her voice was threaded through with sadness. I breathed out a long sigh of relief. I didn't need to take care of Map Girl. Timmon would. The three of us could travel on. We went back to our rooms shortly after dinner to rest and pack.

We turned back into boys that night. The high road beckoned us again! We were setting ourselves free from our lonely, frustrated, persecuted and beaten down, dull, mean little lives where nobody gave a damn about any of us. All that was left back there was misery and a cemetery plot waiting.

Well, while on the road, we'd all become death rebels. Not being religious, we sure as hell weren't going to handle death the way Ardenville did. We talked around in circles about how the churches and people were set on burials and how that worked, and we agreed each one of us was going to give cremation a shot. That being settled, we went forward from there. Maybe we wouldn't have to go back. Now we had a second chance. It was either go back or trust these people to not try to get us locked up or something.

The next morning when dawn broke, we loaded our cars. We were ready to set out on our second road trip.

We watched William pull in with Miss Emma right behind him. She was driving a dark blue 1950 Studebaker 2 R10 Pickup truck. Sturdy and road wise. A good choice. William climbed out of his truck and strolled over to us. He wiped his face with his handkerchief and said, "Emma is taking some art stuff to Tom and the others at the monastery to pave the way for you three."

He shrugged and looked at us nervously. We read between the lines.

"Or else," he said, and rolled his eyes skyward and heaved a sigh.

"I don't know what it is about me and women! Every time I turn around, it seems like another one of them is making me mind some way or another. I get damn...I mean darn... tired of it!"

All four of us men stared at the ground, saddened by the prospect before us. Finally we gave in and accepted our fate. At least it was only one woman. And she was driving her own vehicle. A good one, at that.

"Oh well."

"Well, let's go."

"May as well."

"Yep."

After giving Timmon a handshake and slipping my mother's tiny jewelry box into Map Girl's purse the night before-it felt like the right thing to do, same as when I slipped cash into her purse so many years ago—I was done with all that mushy stuff. I hurried to my car. They waved at us from the front porch as we solemnly caravanned away from the store with Emma following us.

William led the way the first day. When he went too fast, we just let him. Sometimes he pulled off the side of the road and waited for us to catch up. Then he pulled back on in front of us. He wore a beat up cowboy hat, and sometimes we saw him waving it around. We thought we heard him cussing. He said he didn't do it, but we knew all about denial. The town we'd left behind was full of it. William was a troubled man.

Miss Emma ate supper with us each night but left early to go back to her motel room. She said she had stocked up on Twinkies before leaving the ranch.

Knowing my propensity for sticking my foot in my mouth around her, I guarded every word I said. I don't know what Andy and Ben's reasons were, but they watched it, too.

William led again the next day. We followed him through flat, almost barren land. The next couple of days, we caravanned west through Arizona and up into Nevada. That place was old and lonesome, just like us. We crossed Nevada and went up into Oregon and headed north.

The next day after we stopped for lunch, Miss Emma took the lead. We drove through miles of forest until we came to a long driveway. She turned in and we followed her down the driveway. She stopped in front of a large tan building with arched windows and a wide front porch with a dozen wide steps leading up to it.

We parked our vehicles, got out and looked around. A feeling of quiet surrounded us. This was a good place. Andy, Ben, and me waited while William and Miss Emma strolled into the building that looked almost like a church.

All of a sudden, I was plumb worn out. I'd felt guilty over things I didn't have the full story of many times in my life. My inner voice chastised me for it at least once a day. I'd left Map Girl like my mother left me. I knew better, but it hurt to question it. I was damned by guilt. It came with everything I did, and I suspected, always would. It was just part of who I was.

A wave of homesickness washed over me. I wanted to lay down in the back seat of my old Chevy and sleep for a hundred years, then wake up and flee for the home we'd left behind and never leave it again.

I peeked at Ben and Andy to see if they noticed my dark mood. I could see they were stewing in their own bad moods. They looked tired and worn out too. Trying to find a new place to live was wearing all of us out. The work of it kept us stunningly terrified most all the time. Somebody could have slung us in a baby crib or promised us the moon or give us an army to try and make us feel safe, but there was nothing anybody could do that would make us feel truly safe.

Not a church with stained glass windows, for our former town's sanctuaries were riddled with toxic silence and too much misery. We stayed scared every step of the way here. We'd left Ardenville on a mission. But we'd never dreamed of really living our lives in other places. We were not prepared for feeling rootless. We were just beginning to put down roots at the cabin back home when Dan betrayed us and we had to run. But that cabin was only seventy miles from Ardenville. Now we'd traveled three thousand miles from our hometown. And here we stood, waiting for the keys to another cabin.

The good news was, Ardenville was far away. No driving just a few miles to get back there so we could feel safe in our familiar misery. We'd kicked ourselves out of Hell, and now we missed it. I was discovering some of the consequences of taking spontaneous flight. No one is ever completely free of their social and physical environment. I hoped that who we were and where we were mattered somehow in the bigger scheme of things. But we still would never be ready to face the world in the ways other people did. Ben would always read science fiction and Andy would always need to fish. And I would always need a car to tinker with.

We weren't going to change and get all smarmy with other folks. We did not like to get swarmed by other folks. We never wanted to meet anybody new. We mostly didn't like other people. That was our common constant.

Another good part was that we each had enough money and the freedom of choice to insulate ourselves from other people and still follow our inclinations. Money made that possible. In short, we could go or stay. It was up to us.

William and Miss Emma came back out followed by a huge, hefty, sandy-haired fellow dressed in tan slacks and a tan short sleeved shirt. The man glanced at our neatly lined up cars, smiled real big, and changed his course.

"Amazing!" he said with admiration.

He clasped his hands behind his back and circled our cars without touching them. We appreciated that. Then he strolled over to us like nobody ever had a care in the world. I suspected this man knew how to take his time getting through life.

"I'm Brother Tomlinson, Tom for short. Welcome."

We behaved. We knew this part of it must be done. We lined up in a row like prisoners and stated our names and looked him in the eye.

"Bud Spinner."

"Ben Bass."

"Andy Noble."

That was it. As much as we could manage. He clasped his hands behind his back again and circled us like he did with our cars. When he got to the front of us again, he reached out a beefy hand attached to a thick, hairy arm, shook hands with each of us and smiled. Then he turned to William and Miss Emily and handed them keys.

"I'll see you two at dinner tonight," Brother Tom announced in his big, booming voice. Then he turned and strolled back into the main building.

We caravanned to our cabin. There were two small bedrooms. Me and Andy each chose one. Ben got the living room sofa. The cabin had a small living room with a kitchen and a back deck overlooking a small lake and a dock. It was quiet and peaceful. No people around. Any other cabins were hidden from our sight.

It was just like William said. It was very much like our former cabin. We followed William into the village near the monastery and bought groceries, fishing supplies, and books. We settled into the cabin while William and Miss Emma settled into their own place on the monastery grounds. On our first night alone, we ate sandwiches and talked.

"Are we still going back home?" I asked them.

"We need to sleep. We can't think straight right now," Andy growled. "We are too damn tired to start the trip back home right now anyway."

We went to bed. It wasn't even dark out. We didn't care. We were exhausted. The world out there had backed us into another corner. We would figure out what to do about it later. Ben slept on the hideaway tucked inside the living room couch.

We ate and slept and read and fished and pondered on it for close to a week. William left us a note on the front door telling us where to find him if we needed anything. Other than that, we didn't see him or Miss Emma or anybody else.

"This is our first long trip away from home. Maybe we can get over not planning it better?" Andy said.

"You make it sound like we're just on vacation instead of leaving back there for good!" Ben growled at Andy.

We were sitting around the living room, arguing about going back. We talked a little about it every night after supper. Tonight was our fifth night of sorting it out. But Ben was through talking.

"I don't care a damn about going back. I don't want to. I feel better away from there! And we have got better. Bud, your vocabulary has expanded. Now you can do more than grunt when people speak to you. Andy, you've learned more about other fishing places and other kinds of fish, and I've found new books to read. I say we stay together wherever we land at."

Andy and I looked at each other. Ben didn't care about going back. He just wanted to stay with us wherever we went.

Snow squalls are localized in time and location.

Ćhapter Twelve

The next day, a note appeared on the cabin door. It was for me. "To Bud Spinner," the note read, "Come to the main house to take a phone call at two o'clock from Map Girl."

I got ready to go up to the main house to wait for the call. Ben and Andy raised their eyebrows at my choice of clothes. I was wearing black slacks, a black shirt with colorful cactus on it, and silver-tipped black Cordovan shoes.

"Fancy!" Ben and Andy said. Andy whistled.

"Who knows who's up there?" I said. "Best to be prepared."

Brother Tom met me in the foyer of the main building. "Good afternoon!"

He clasped his hands behind his back and circled me. When he got back to the front, he smiled at me with his mouthful of large, even teeth. I followed him through the foyer. The foyer led into a large room with high ceilings. The furniture looked expensive and well used. I thought I recognized two of Miss Emma's paintings among those on the walls.

The phone was in an office just off the community living room. Brother Tom waved at a chair behind a desk before he went out and closed the door behind him. I looked at my watch. I was very early, as usual. I was always early to my appointments. I was early for school and work all of my life. Then William walked in and sat down.

"I just stopped by to mention a couple of things before Map Girl calls. She is a Psychic you know. And a Sensitive. A person who knows things regular people don't pick up on?"

"I know."

"She's one of the smartest people you will ever meet, just in her own way. She has helped us all out with her Sight when the occasion called for it. I figure she wants to help you. Or she wouldn't have called and set this up."

I didn't answer.

William stood up and said, "I just wanted you to know before you talked with her. Don't laugh at her or be skeptical in any way okay? That would not be good."

He left. The phone rang. I stared at it awhile. Finally I picked up the receiver.

"Hello?"

It was Map Girl. I'd know her voice anywhere.

"It's Bud Spinner here," I said cautiously.

"How are you, Bud?" she asked joyfully. "Did you three wise men enjoy your trip?"

"It was okay."

"Are you settling in?"

I didn't know how to answer that question except with the truth.

"We might go back home."

"No! You can't do that!" she shouted.

I jerked my ear away from the phone.

I heard the phone change hands. A man cleared his throat loudly into the receiver. I jerked my ear away again.

"Hello?" he said.

I knew that voice. It was time to hang up. The receiver was on its way down when I stopped and slowly put it back to my ear.

"What did you say?"

"This is Dan. Dan Swain!" he shouted. "Damn it man, I got news for you! And it ain't good! Listen to me, okay?"

"What news?"

"A bunch of teenagers burnt your garage to the ground. All that's left is ashes!"

I took that in for a minute.

"Anything else?"

Dan went to shouting, and I heard Map Girl grab the phone away from him.

"Now you hold on just a minute, Bud Spinner. I got some news for you, too," she said in a firm voice.

A long silence with Dan shouting from farther and farther away ran down the line. Map Girl's voice came back on the line.

"You are one of the Three Magi. Like the ones in the Bible stories. You three men came here to give three gifts to people who need them. You have given me mine. Now Andy and Ben must give their gifts. They can't think about leaving until they do.

Here's what you all have been.

Grouchy.

Crotchety.

Crabby.

Cranky.

Obtuse.

Irascible.

Ornery.

Truculent.

Surly."

Map Girl said, "Your garage burned down so you would not have anything to go back to. No roots. That is a bad damned place, and I should know. You got away too. So you should count your blessings instead of mourning the loss of evil like it's the end of the world. You better not try to talk Andy and Ben into going back to Hell. That would be really bad news for them. Lousy karma."

I started to speak, but Map Girl interrupted me.

"First things first. Get off your ass and sign that cabin back there over to Dan. He needs it for his children and his own future, and you need to be free of it. Then you go to Miss Emma and apologize for your bad behavior toward her, and volunteer Ben to sit for a painting. Next you find William the Dude, and you two get a dark green wood rowboat, the old fashioned kind, and oars and a good camera for Andy. Paint the boat green if you have to. Do it exactly like I said and in that order. We will talk more about you guy's marvelous charm and personalities later."

She took another breath and went on.

"Some things aren't going to change. For now, just eat more oranges. I'll have more directions to give you later. Andy and Ben's gifts have to be given, and you have to help them do it. Just be glad I have a liking for all things aged and rustic. That's all. I'm done."

Map Girl sighed and hung up. I stared at the phone until the dial tone came on, then I hung up too. I sat there awhile and played with the letter opener and the stopwatch laying on the desk. Then I stood up and wandered out into the living room or whatever the Brothers called it. I looked at all the paintings on the walls, especially Miss Emma's.

Why did Map Girl want me to volunteer Ben for a painting? I was to apologize to Miss Emma? Green rowboats and cameras? So that cute little Map Girl, so sweet and quiet, knew cusswords? How about that! Suddenly I needed a wrench in my hand and a car waiting with the hood up. And I needed a beer. Badly.

In the end, I did everything Map Girl instructed me to do. I started right then. I searched out Miss Emma while I was still dressed up nice. Dressing up was a hassle. I didn't want to have to do it again later today. Once was enough.

Miss Emma was staying in a home tucked into the side of a hill. I apologized to her for bothering her and offered Ben up as a sitter, like Map Girl told me to.

"Map Girl told me to do it."

I felt like I was offering Ben up as a sacrificial lamb on an unknown altar without him knowing it. I felt like a traitor when all I did was put on my black shoes to go take a telephone call. Miss Emma thought about what I told her. Ben, Andy, and I were three introverted personalities. That's how we could get along so well. We knew the flavors of each other's silences. I was learning Miss Emma's.

She said Ben was not to come alone. She wanted all three of us. Three sacrificial lambs. Miss Emma was cool and crisp with me. We set the time for his first sitting at ten the next morning. I wandered back to the cabin and changed clothes before I gave Andy and Ben the glad tidings. I just knew they would jump up and down with joy about it.

"What the hell have you been doing all day?" Andy asked.

"Did you get your phone call?" Ben asked.

"Since when did we become cute enough to sit for a famous painter?" Andy added.

"You mean artist, not painter," I said.

Andy scratched his head.

"We'll go, but not because of you. We'll go because we don't want to make Miss Emma any madder than she already is at us."

They each grabbed a beer and huffed their way out to the back deck to stare at the water.

We arrived at Miss Emma's house at ten o'clock on the dot. Miss Emma slid the glass doors open for us, turned and walked away. She was dressed in some sort of white coverall. We trailed her into her studio. The room was huge, empty and very tall and full of sunlight pouring through large windows. Big blank canvases were stacked against one wall. Paper and pencils, paint and brushes and pens and other things lay on a long thin desk against a wall. A lemon-colored yellow sofa stood in the middle of the studio. She motioned to us to sit on the sofa. The sofa was small, and we had to crowd up against each other.

Miss Emma set a large white canvas against the wall in front of us. Then she circled us and walked back and forth looking at us for awhile. I hoped she was seeing something good. Suddenly, there was a large brush in her hand and she was dipping red paint out of a jar and spreading it on the canvas with the brush.

"Freeze!" she commanded when Andy moved. We knew how to freeze. Frozen was something we were experienced in. I had "frozen" many times in my childhood and later too. I froze in the hall closet in the old house when my dad stomped by. I froze every time mother banged a pot in the kitchen.

Ben froze in the park in the winter to keep from going home. The words in his books warmed him just enough to keep him insulated from his family's hate and wrath. Their meanness to him fell upon ice. Frozen. Yep. Andy fished in the summer and ice fished for his wishes under a lake layered over with ice too thick to have anything bad under the water during the winter.

Miss Emma kept painting. The canvas filled with wide reds and strong oranges of anger. The coldness of our rage crept onto the canvas when she tossed a small tin of dark blue and white marbled paint on a corner of the canvas.

She was an abstract painter. I'd read about them. That stuff on the canvas was us. That was what we looked like to her. Our collective anger and rage applied with the sweeping motions of rejection and distance, looked like that to her. Ben began to weep quietly. I looked at him, astounded.

"Get out," Miss Emma ordered. She looked at Andy and me, quiet and calm like, as though she was just reminding us of what time it was. Shocked, we stood up and walked out. As we left, we heard Ben start babbling to Miss Emma about himself.

"Lord, help us!" I muttered to Andy and shook my head. Blabbermouth Ben was on the loose again! This was going to be far worse than I imagined. Miss Emma painting us, using us as a sacrifice to her art, was at least honorable and something we could stand. But Ben turning into a blabbing, crying mess right in front of her! *There was no honor in it,* I thought bitterly.

Snowmelt is surface runoff produced from melting snow.

Chapter Thirteen

I watched Bud and Andy leave. I kept on babbling. Miss Emma kept on painting while I talked.

"I've been through hell all of my life. That's just all there is to it. I have made too many mistakes. It would take me forty lifetimes to rectify them. Or more. I can say that all my life I have been so damn dumb and mad at the world and God, that I didn't understand or even see the sweet possibilities life kept laying before me until they were all gone. I have always had too much arrogance, a short sighted ego, and I am easily manipulated and tricked. And fooled. And hated.

I wish I could have loved more and better. I have been bitter and filled with resentments many lengthy times. I have been stupid and mean mouthed. I have let others suffer and declared it had nothing to do with me. Until years later when the awareness of what I did caught up with me.

I have just about died from remorse three hundred and thirty two times. I write it down. Keep track of it. Every time something new comes in about a wrong I have done to someone, it kicks my ass all over again. Knocks me down. The only good thing is that my fear is less than it used to be. It got worn down somehow. Wore out, maybe.

My fear was so high that for years, I didn't know anyone else existed in the world. I just kept looking at me, trying to keep from screaming. Trying to fix it. I'm a creep, and a no good louse. That's what my large, estranged family says about me. That I am one weird guy. That I do stuff that's way left of center."

I looked at Miss Emma beseechingly. I was crying and saying stuff I didn't even know about myself. I was horrified at my outburst. But Miss Emma just kept on painting. She moved on to another canvas while I kept on spilling my guts. Black and grays crisscrossing each other making high points up at the top of the canvas. Just some paint. But it carried a suggestion of a male, big-knuckled hand holding up each point at the top. Like a tent. A black tent. With somebody crying underneath.

Miss Emma didn't turn from painting. She added deep purple above the black. Here and there. It wasn't random. It looked right. It made sense to me. Miss Emma was painting the secret, chronic emotional pain I have always felt. She was sweeping it up into the air and onto a canvas. The pain and hurt on the canvas was dark and raw and obvious. A simple man's simple fear-filled hurt. Young. And disabled with it. Shut down a long time ago. Sad and knowing this and can't accept it.

I cried myself empty. When I became aware of my surroundings again, Miss Emma said curtly, "Get out. Ten o'clock tomorrow morning."

She turned on her heel and left.

I looked at the two paintings leaning on the wall in front of me. Large, stark and full of emotions, the paintings were brilliant and breathtaking. One was done in shades of reds and oranges. Anger and hurt clearly on view. The other held the hidden stuff under black and gray with purple and suggestions of flesh colored hands holding the dark world above from falling in on a suffering human being. That stuff on the canvas was finally out of me. Not in me anymore. But I didn't feel it. It was not over yet.

I walked back to the cabin. Andy and Bud left me to my own devices. I was hungry, so I ate and went to the back porch and sat down and began remembering.

I'd always craved to be loved by my family, but it never happened What did happen was cruelty, meanness, jealousy, beatings, and hunger. My family defended their wrongs to the death of love or like. They wanted me to learn how to do it too.

The only solution I ever came up with was isolation and books to keep from turning out like them. Books were a doorway to my imagination, allowed because nobody could see it, and I didn't tell about it, either. Rended apart by family horrors day after day, I needed the hospital rest provided by the soothing, interesting books I read. Little by little, I healed each time, resolutely using reading and isolation as my prescription.

No turning to girls or having a bunch of pals for me. No desire to make a "better" marriage when I grew up, or to raise "better" kids. My future was to be alone. I sorted through life and chose good books to read. Especially science books and science fiction. They let me enter a different world; one where the bad guys got theirs.

I met Andy in grade school. We immediately recognized each other's plight and went our way together. Two isolates avoiding as much of life out there as we could. We both liked a couple of girls in high school, but nothing panned out. We never talked about it. We took up bowling and we liked old cars. We went to school by working nights and got degrees and worked at the same place. We rented houses and stayed friends. That was all until we met Bud.

We met him on purpose. He never knew it, still doesn't. We both developed the habit of listening carefully to the gossip circulating around town, not participating, just monitoring it for any sign of trouble.

We heard stuff about Bud from time to time. People said he was an odd duck that kept to himself. They wouldn't have anything to do with him except for the fact that he was the best damn mechanic in the state. Maybe in the whole county. They said he was a complete grease monkey. Cars were the only thing on his mind, and it showed. He had dirt and grease on him every time they saw him. They laughed and ignored him other than when they needed gas or something repaired on their vehicles.

We crossed Bud's path a few times over the years and figured out he might be like us. That day in the rain, we found out. He was like us. We weren't alone anymore. Now there were three of us to fend off the world together. The Three Musketeers of Isolation.

Now, about the music. I never liked the latest songs the kids at school liked. Junk about love and such. I kept my eyes looking down most of the time. I had a good reason for doing it. I never told anybody about my problem. Here's what it was, and still is. I can't help but react to certain pieces of classical music. I don't know anything about classical music, and I don't know the names of the pieces that work me over the most. When I hear the right song or whatever they call it, I weep, I hold my hands up to the sky and look to heaven. I make sounds and pace around like a fool. Now that's all okay when I am alone, but if anybody else is around, it doesn't look too good on me. I do the same thing with certain kinds of art. I never know which art will throw me into a kind of bliss in which I might do foolish things.

Andy likes Big Band and Swing music and Bud likes to listen to baseball games on his car radio. But me, I hide my secret from them, and it is pretty easy to do because art galleries and operas are not a common part of our lives. If there is a promise of ever reaching the god within the self, I go there every time I hear certain music or see certain art pieces, things created by human beings. By people, of which I am one.

Miss Emma knew about my inner ways. I don't know how she knew about that, but she did. Probably from past lives together, that's what Bud says. We can't learn it all in this classroom of life on just one trip through. That's what he tells us to explain how the deal works here. I guess I believe in reincarnation. A whole lot of other people in this world believe in it. It is the only time template that makes any sense at all, and, it may be the only way a whole bunch of us manage to get through life, scientifically speaking.

Anyways, the day after I graduated from high school, I moved out and never looked back. Old Mr. Farther took me in, and I lived with him in the little cranny in the church basement they rented to him. I got a job and an old car and went to college forty miles away. The basement apartment was a poor excuse of a place, but we fared well together, and Mr. Farther stayed quiet and proud of me.

After I got a job, I rented a nice house on the end of town and moved him into it. He puttered around in the back yard and grew tomatoes and made me mayonnaise and bologna sandwiches for lunch. I didn't like them, but I ate them anyway to please him. He didn't live long after I moved him in with me. He didn't have anybody, and the church people never came to see him, so I paid for a fine suit and a good funeral for him.

The church women finally offered to put on a lunch for his funeral, but I just give them an awful look and turned away. Five people came to his funeral. He wasn't a big shot or a relative of anybody in town. I found out later that he was an old drunk who wandered into town when he was middle-aged and stayed. Nobody knew more than that about him. They never bothered. I took his picture while he was out back working in the garden in better days. He smiled at me and held up a rutabaga he'd just pulled from the ground. I carry that picture with me.

Someday, I might try to find out more about old Mr. Farthers. Maybe a detective like "Traitor Dan" could find his family. Then I could tell them where he is, so they wouldn't worry. Old Mr. Farther's memory is just like the music and the art to me. He was my only father. I better shut up now. Bud and Andy call me blabbermouth Ben, but I don't mind.

High mountain snowmelt runs downhill.

Chapter Fourteen

Andy and I didn't say anything to Ben about his breakdown. But for the first time, we didn't run. From this place or him. Or talk about running. A new day had dawned. What the hell was happening to us? Maybe we didn't run because Miss Emma didn't try to connect to any of us. Even Ben. She just kept on painting as though her life depended on it while he blabbed his guts out.

We didn't talk at all that night. The next morning we stayed silent. Nobody wanted breakfast. Just coffee. We were on time for our ten o'clock appointment with Miss Emma. We were bleary eyed from lack of sleep and very cranky.

"If she thinks she's going do that to me too, she's dead wrong," Andy muttered to me as Ben rushed ahead of us into her studio.

I ignored Andy's words. I stopped and put my hands on my hips and shook my head and watched Ben. Now when did Ben ever rush towards anything? He was supposed to run away, not towards. That's what we all did. Run away. Not toward things.

Miss Emma parked us like cars on the lemon colored sofa again and started to work on a fresh canvas. She started out with blue. Everywhere blue. Sad blue.

Ben ignored us and started explaining his life to her again. Andy and I rolled our eyes at each other, and then upward. We were completely mortified, but we stayed put because we didn't know what the hell else to do.

Ben blathered on with his whining and pity party life. He tried to drag me and Andy into it on the start.

"I was meant to land here. To stay here the rest of my life. Oh, not forever, for I believe in reincarnation after Bud explained it in detail. I've read more and learned more than just science fiction. I've read crime novels that would scare the socks off of you. I've read stories telling all about the malicious treatment of women down through time. Damn glad I ain't one. I've traveled the world with spies and countesses and robbers through books. I've read romances, trying to find a formula to make it possible for me to have a spouse or a lady companion, anything. But nothing ever worked. I have accepted that I am an unqualified loner."

He looked at Andy, then at me.

"Not alone. Just alone with two other loners."

He looked at Miss Emma again.

Andy and I looked at each other.

"Freeze!" Miss Emma ordered. I did. Then I zoned out in self defense, hearing only parts of Ben's continuing pity party confessions.

"I look back over my life, blah blah... guilty as sin... didn't help my sister...chastised her and her children...blah blah blah....asshole that I was, I didn't see it.... I was pissy and self-righteous... I was mean...I cannot undo or redo the things I did... blah blah... live in remorse... apologize... too late.... won't allow myself to.... blah blah blah... ever have another... I am not well liked.... I am a loner... least contact possible with... blah blah..."

"Stop snoring, Bud!" Miss Emma ordered. I jerked myself up from my slumped position and listened to Ben.

"Remorse and pity have been my unquestioned way of thinking for many years. But last night for the first time, after I did my nightly recapitulation of all the bad things I did, something else came up. I heard myself say, 'Well, everybody does stuff wrong. It's part of the trip. So, get over it. Stop this eternal pity party!'

I already told myself that a thousand times. But this time I knew I could do it. I will accept that I have been an ignorant, cruel asshole this lifetime. I have done others harm. But what the hell did I expect, coming out of the family I did into the world, all angry and pissed off at God and people, not knowing anything, and being trained to use maliciousness to deal with people? It hasn't been about forgiving myself, it has been about understanding myself first, then the forgiveness happens. I have been doing it all out of order. Last night I started reordering my life...."

"Get out," Miss Emma interrupted his words. Andy and I rushed the door. Ben just sat there.

"All of you," she said. Ben got up and followed us out the door.

"Be here again at ten tomorrow morning. All of you."

Andy and I hurried ahead of Ben on our way back to the cabin. He was still blabbing. We parked him out on the back deck with beer and chips. He didn't try to get us to stay and listen while he kept on pouring his guts out. We checked on him later and he'd finally wound down to fits and starts. That was a good sign. That meant he might stop blathering on and shut up soon. He asked me to bring him more beer and grill him a couple burgers.

"Not 'til you shut the hell up. And maybe not then."

"But I can't help myself, Bud."

"The hell you can't!"

I turned on my heel and went back inside. Awhile later, it started to rain. A light drizzle. Andy and I went and got the now sleeping, comatose figure of Ben the Blabber, helped him inside, and parked him in a bedroom and shut the door on him. Just in case. No sofa or wandering around for Blabby Ben tonight. We didn't see him until the next morning when he came out for breakfast.

"I'm hungry as a bear!" he announced.

Andy and I had nothing to say. We pulled our plates filled with our hearty breakfast of eggs, toast, bacon and hash browns to ourselves. There was none for Ben.

He strolled to the fridge, opened the door, pulled out a bunch of leftovers and put them on the counter. Then he went into some serious eating. By that time, Andy and I were done with our breakfasts. We marched the plates and so forth to the sink and dumped them in it. Clean up later. Then we turned our backs on him and left him to it.

We arrived at Miss Emma's studio at ten on the dot. Ben rushed ahead of us, as usual. Andy and I glanced at each other mournfully. It was to be expected. Sadly, we took our places again on the lemon colored sofa. If there was ever a lemon that deserved to be stuck on a lemon colored sofa, it was Ben, not us.

Miss Emma started painting. We waited for Ben's onslaught of words. Another giant pity party of grand proportions flowing from him. But no. He sat there, quiet and smiling. At last Ben had shut up. Andy and I let out huge gusts of relief.

We watched Miss Emma move into softer, lighter hues of blue instead of the storms she slashed across the horizon of the canvas the day before.

"I need to tell you something," Miss Emma spoke into the silence. Then she started spilling her guts! Andy and I rolled our eyes heavenward. Oh God, does it never end? I didn't know how much more I could take of this. I looked over at Andy.

"I didn't understand either," she said. "I thought it required my mother for me to have an understanding of life, and she died when I was two. I thought she took that knowledge with her. That it died along with her. Father has propped me up with his Equanimity for all of my life. Then Ray was born, and that held me steady for the longest time. He was a gift from a beautiful and merry stranger who sought nothing but the fulfillment of joy in his life. He couldn't stay because I knew not that territory.

Then father married that Mafia woman, that religious fanatic and moved to California, and Ray married Geena and moved to Carolina, and Celia is only here once in awhile. I stay lonesome and empty, so I paint all the time. It helps fill me up."

Miss Emma stopped painting. She grabbed a rag and wiped her hands off. Her face was wet and red and raw. The blue painting behind her was filled with swirls that beckoned us to take part in its misery, quiet, peace, and joy. Ben's usual look of despondency and wariness disappeared. He looked serene.

Instinctively, I knew Miss Emma was finished with me and Andy. Andy turned and run out the door with me right behind him. It was way too smarmy in there for us.

After Ben's experience, which Andy and I were forced to suffer through, I was beginning to dread Map Girl's words about more "gifts". Andy's "gift" was next. A good camera, she had said, a green rowboat, and oars. God, I hoped Andy wouldn't have to do his own peculiar version of confession like Blabbermouth Ben did! I didn't know how much of that junk I could stand!

I would need William the Dude's help. He was the camera buff. I hurried off to find him.

Water from snow melt is a needed part of the water cycle.

Ćhapter Fifteen

Ben had turned into a sobbing blabbermouth, and Andy had run away. I needed to find William. For some reason, I stayed in a hurry lately, and couldn't stop myself.

"Damn it!" I muttered under my breath. "I need to start carrying a wrench in my hand everywhere I go! That would calm me down. But wouldn't that make me look like a crazed attacker or killer?"

What was a man supposed to do when he reached his limit?

"I'll think about it later," I muttered. One thing kept sticking in my mind. We would all be what we were, no matter how hard we tried not to be. Our world was a miserable prison with a nonstop vineyard of bitter, fearful roots supporting our uneasy positions. Life was supposed to be easier when one hid out in a cabin in a secluded monastery, wasn't it? That hadn't happened so far. I muttered some more, a thing I was doing a lot of lately.

William was lounging on the porch of a small, nondescript white house. He was doing nothing. He looked peaceful. Calm and laid back. Relaxed. I rushed the one porch step and slapped my butt down on it with my back to him. I didn't want him to see the desperate look on my face. I didn't want any more adventure, intimacy, or authentic communication. I didn't mind my needs staying unmet forever. I just wanted to be left alone.

But I was being forced to do this. Map Girl had ordered it, and I suspected that the wrath of God wasn't as powerful as hers would be if I didn't do it.

"Okay."

I tossed the word into the air, figuring that William the Dude would hear it and become alert instead of lounging like a rope of white haired spaghetti across his chair.

"Ben is at Miss Emma's being painted, blabbing his fool guts out and crying. So is she. Blabbing her guts out, I mean. Miss Emma. They are both confessing their sins and stuff."

"Map Girl put me up to this."

I announced bitterly. "It's all her fault."

"My garage burned down. Me and Andy and Ben's stuff was stored in it. Now we got nothing. You're the one that told me to listen to Map Girl. She says I got to get Andy a green rowboat, a good camera and some oars. And she said you got to help."

I stated this last part with vicious satisfaction. William the Dude may as well be in this mess with me.

"Maybe you better start at the front of your story," he said in a mild, unruffled voice.

"Well, it all started with that phone call from Map Girl."

When I finished telling it, I said, "And we might or might not sign the former cabin over to that liar Dan Swain."

"Where's Andy now?" he asked. I shrugged. He stood up and went in the house. In a minute he came back out carrying a camera case. I could tell it was an expensive one.

"Well, let's go find him," he said easily.

We found Andy sitting on the end of the dock with a fishing line dangling in the water. He jumped up as we approached and stuck the palm of his hand out toward us as if to ward off evil.

"Stay back!" he shouted, glassy eyed. "I don't want to have to jump in the water because I can't swim, okay? So stay back! Go away! I've had enough!"

We stopped where we were. William the Dude said, "Andy, do you like to take photos? I heard you did. What do like to take photos of?"

Andy blinked at him and put his hand down.

"Yeah. I do. Black and whites. Pictures of just about anything. But not much of people. Just some of Ben and Bud."

"You could take pictures of people and get close to them that way. You could set up a dark room and take all the pictures you wanted and develop them. Then you could look at them all you wanted to without talking to 'em."

"Wouldn't that be a switch," Andy snarled sarcastically. He turned his back to us and stared out over the water. William the Dude walked a little closer, then carefully set the camera down where Andy could see it.

"I've got a little book of instructions if you need it."

Andy laid the fishing rod down and picked up the camera case and opened it. He took the camera out of it and examined it. Then he asked William the Dude a few quick questions that I didn't understand.

After he answered Andy's questions, William the Dude said, "There's a bowling alley over in Quickstone. Not many people go there. It's a little place. They got the best chili cheese fries and burgers in all of Oregon. And the bowling ain't too bad, either. Want to go this afternoon? Say, about two o'clock? You can let Ben know about it, too."

At two o'clock, me and Blabbermouth Ben and Picture Taking Andy and William the Zen Dude set out for Quickstone. Andy brought William the Dude's camera along. We bowled and Andy took pictures. We ate chili cheese dogs and Andy took pictures. We drank beer and Andy took pictures. Of everyone and everything, while Ben bowled and ate and drank beer and basked in his newly achieved, greatly relieved and now empty interior. Ben said a bunch of nonsense I couldn't understand, and never wanted to.

"Now I can reconfigure my internal government, and I am currently pondering the appointees for each position. How many positions do I need? Should they be vetted? One term or two? How many years? Do I need Senators or just congressmen? Term limits?"

"Lord help us!" I muttered.

When we got back to the cabin, William the Dude said, "Why don't you three stay here for awhile? It will be good for you. I took care of the camera part. You get the rowboat and oars, Bud. Me and Miss Emma are heading back to the ranch in the morning. I will see you again in about three weeks. Or you can come back with us."

Dumbfounded, we stared at him. He spread out his large, bony hands in a pacifying gesture.

"This is what I think. You are the three wise men, the three Magi. You know, like in Biblical terms? Your gifts have been given, as far as I know. If they haven't, too damn... I mean too darn bad. You three belong in a monastery, like priests, a place where it is peaceful and quiet with expected routines and no calls upon you to be emotional with other people.

You already know that, right? And from what I've heard of your stories, you three always have had a propensity for aloneness that would make the tallest snow capped mountain shudder."

He grinned.

"I also know it was because of your upbringings. You escaped from a place that was wrong for you, and now this may be the right place for all of you, who knows? Try to stay and give this place and the way they do things here a chance, okay? Then you'll know better about what you really need. Personally, I think all three of you are innocents who can't calculate algebra any better than Map Girl can. You have helped us all immensely and in ways I know you don't see. But I do. So do others. You will be well treated and very respected and honored here.

In this place there is room for you to let down your guard and learn and heal. I know you guys are not the lovey-dovey types. Never will be. So don't be afraid, because here, you don't have to get close to anybody. The brothers are not demonstrative. So relax and I will see you in three weeks."

We stayed. The three weeks sped by. With each passing day we fell back more into our old ways. And we accepted them. Some things changed and others not. We would always be fearful. We had gotten better at connecting, but none of us would ever like it.

The Brothers never let anyone in that wasn't supposed to be at the monastery. The hidden gates were there, and surprisingly, it made us feel good. Nobody from the old place could just walk in on us. Including Dan Swain. Oops! We'd forgot! We put in a hasty call to the store. William the Dude answered.

"Hello?"

"Does Dan Swain know where we are?" I asked without preamble. After a few seconds William answered.

"Nope."

"Good!"

"Why?"

"We don't ever want to see or talk to that traitor again!"

"I thought Map Girl said you were signing the cabin over to him."

"She did. But we've talked it over, and we're not going to do it. It's our cabin, and it happened to all of us. The betrayal, I mean. Dan Swain's a private eye. He can find us easy and show up here any time."

"We don't want to ever see him again."

We waited while a long silence spun out over the phone connection.

"Okay. A lawyer could put this right. It would maybe take a judge, too."

"What do you mean?"

"Well, you could sign the cabin over to him with certain conditions put in place legally. If he breaks the conditions, then he forfeits the cabin. One of the

conditions could be that he never comes near any of
you again"

"That might work."

"Okay. I'll get started on it."

"Okay." We hung up.

By the time William the Dude returned, we had
decided to accept the ways of our new world. We
would not apologize for who we were. We never did
that, even before we broke free of the bondage that
held us in its clutches for so long.

This monastery living was beginning to look pretty
good. A place protected from the usual world. A
hideout. So what if we weren't religious? We didn't
have to participate in any of that stuff to stay here.
And the little brewery held its own kind of charm.
The smells coming from it drifted over our cabin, and
the beer was excellent. Things were to the point that
me and Ben and Andy were thinking and speaking in
more than three word sentences.

William the Dude arrived on Sunday afternoon.
The lawyer and judge arrived together on Wednesday
afternoon. They questioned us, then we signed all of
the legal documents. The cabin would belong to Dan
Swain and his children. But he would have to work
for it. He would have to keep an eye on Ben and
Andy's families and send us six month reports like
he once did for Map Girl.

The cabin reverted back to me or Ben or Andy at
any time any one of us so chose. Dan was to stay
away from us. No spying, no 'accidental' meetings, no
correspondence, nothing. Everything was to go to a
post office box near William the Dude's residence in
California. William's staff would keep us informed

from there. We signed the documents. Next they would be sent to Dan to sign. The lawyer suggested Andy and Ben write a short letter home to their families. After all, somebody might decide to get worried about them and try to search them out.

The lawyer said, "Since you're getting older, they may begin to think that when you die, if there is anything left, it should go to them. That's a big incentive for a lot of people to hunt somebody down."

"What do we say in the letter?" Andy asked.

"Both letters need to be a little bit different. From what I've heard about your backgrounds, I would advise notifying somebody that you are not coming back, that you are selling everything you ever owned there, that you have no money, whether you do or not. Tell them that all three of you have moved to California and are now beach bums. Keep it short and simple. William can send the letters to a friend of his in northern California to be mailed, so they get a California postmark that isn't anywhere close to where William lives."

We wrote the letters right then. They looked them over, we sealed them up, and William pocketed them. We were now officially beach bums. Then we talked about the garage property. The lawyer would see to the sale of it. With it gone, we would have no roots, nothing left back in Ardenville.

William sent us the signed contract from Dan Swain in a couple of weeks. We bought a new lock box and placed the legal papers in it. The burned down garage property sold quickly and we put the contract from the sale in the lockbox, too. We covered all the bases we knew how to cover. We'd moved our money, our lives, our habits and ourselves out of reach, so we hoped.

145

Too rapid a snow melt can cause flooding.

$\mathcal{C}$hapter Sixteen

Ben and I found Andy a new wood rowboat and painted it green, cussing all the way through the damn paint job. After it dried and "cured" so it wouldn't sink and cause Andy to drown, he took it out on the small lake. He paddled out with his new oars and took pictures with his new camera. He wore a lifejacket. A small, inflatable raft lay on the seat beside of him. Moored at the dock was the smaller, plain rescue boat Andy had insisted on, in case we needed to rescue him.

We watched him bobbing out on the water and waited. Nothing happened. Lightning didn't strike. No voice that sounded like Map Girl came from above to announce, "The last gift has been given! Now hie' Ye' homeward!"

Ben and I painted a few words on a board with the leftover green paint and stuck the sign in the ground near the dock. It read, "Loonies in the Boonies Lake." Then we went back to the cabin, strolled out on the back deck, broke the tabs on a couple of brews, sat down and watched Andy.

*

The monastery had an auto repair shop the size of a warehouse. It was filled with everything from tractors to cars that needed repairing. The garage was located behind a screen of evergreens at the north end of the grounds.

There was a fine, big library right off of the living room in the main house, and Brother Tom told us we could use it any time. He said it was hardly ever used, because everyone worked in the gardens or took care of livestock or groomed the grounds.

Andy went with Brother Tom to see the gardens. He took pictures of the gardens. Andy took up sleeping with his camera. He said it was because he might wake up and find something interesting in black and white. Andy added gardening to his fishing and photography. He was better at the gardening than he was at the fishing. Ben was spending time journaling in the library. I was learning about tractor engines in the garage.

Sometimes we ate with the Brothers. They chanted prayers softly before and after meals. I didn't pay any attention to their words on purpose, for I didn't want to disagree with them, but the sound of their words was comforting.

*

Andrew Noble

When I was a kid, my older brother Miles boxed my ears all the time. He held his hands apart, slapped them over my ears and laughed. My ears popped like mad and hurt. I was afraid I would lose my hearing, and mostly I did.

Ben and Bud didn't know I could barely hear what they said. I didn't give any of any of the signals of being hard of hearing because my brothers threatened me out of it. They threatened me out of being curious too. It got so I wasn't curious about

anything. I didn't know what was going on, so I tried
to smarten up in other ways.

There was another problem too. When I fished, I
was forced to deal with the inner ear problems
caused by the ear boxing I'd endured for years. I sat
out there on the water and watched it move. I could
hardly hear it, so I watched it move and change
colors and talk to its members, the waves. People
didn't like my staring at them. The waves were like
people I didn't have to look away from. I could take
my time and study them out.

Another brother, Ernest, five years older than me,
kept almost drowning me so I couldn't look beneath
the water ever again without seeing his face. That's
why I go to the water. He spent many times during
the three summers he babysat us when I was seven,
eight, and nine, almost drowning me and my three
sisters while my two oldest brothers drove by and
laughed at us. That's why I can't swim.

Friday nights when our parents came in from
work with their paychecks cashed, they handed him
over a good amount for babysitting. We came to hate
them as much as we did him.

He did two things to us.

There was a creek full of cattails, high weeds, and
black leeches past the field back of our house. Ernest
waited until our parents went to work. Then he lined
us up and made us follow him to the creek. He stood
over us on the creek bank and forced us into the
filthy black water. He made us stand in the water up
to our necks until we were covered with filthy black
leeches. Then he let us out and disappeared while we

cried and took sticks and scraped the swollen leeches off of each other.

In the afternoon, he marched us down to the bridge that crossed that same creek at a wide spot in the gravel road. Ernest was very industrious when it was something he wanted to do. He was industrious with us, and with making himself a swimming hole under the bridge crossing the creek. He cleaned it all out and deepened his swimming hole. There was sand along it and no weeds or leeches. He made us go under the bridge and stand on the bank and watch while he made each one of us, one at a time, get in his swimming hole.

"You can do it!" he either cajoled or yelled, depending on his mood.

"Come on in!"

"You ain't afraid, are you?" he would laugh and grin, his wide mouth open, his big teeth gleaming like he was going to bite us.

"You don't have to be afraid. I'll take care of you. I'm just gonna' teach you to swim. That's all."

The he'd grab one of us and pull us into the deep water and hold us down under it until our air was gone and we were getting ready to suck in water. He stayed under the water in front of us and watched our faces and grinned. I have never forgotten his face under the water. He told us, "I would drown every damn one of you, but they would get me for murder, and I don't aim to go to prison for the likes of you. None of you should have ever been born. That bitch should have stopped with me!"

Ernest loved the water and he was a good swimmer. If he'd been any lazier about regular work, he would have been dead long before he died years later in a fiery car accident. The idea of him being burned to a crisp never bothered me one minute. It was a timely cremation as far as I was concerned.

I left home and moved in with Mr. Prinzeton and his big, happy family when I was sixteen. I stayed out of their way, washed the dishes and set out the garbage. I lived with them until I finished high school and went away to college on a scholarship. Ben and I had similar families. That gave us our strong connection. We could understand each other's plight without words. We met when we were in grade school and stayed friends. Eventually, we both ended up with engineering degrees and working at the same factory in town.

God never figured in our equations. He had failed us. We lived in rent houses at opposite ends of town, worked and stayed confirmed bachelors and best friends. No joyful kids and smug wives. The idea of doing that gig gave both of us the shudders. We had endured enough of our own personal family lives, enough to last us a lifetime. But our strongest connection went beyond blood or race. It was fear. We were unconditional with each other. And we bowled.

For a long time, I avoided thinking about the old days at all. Then over time, I became more able to look at what happened, in bits and pieces. It was a horror story, regardless of my parents making light of it when we got older and confronted them about it. Dorothy and Gene Noble never wavered in their denial of what Ernest really was.

I can't swim, so I stay on the surface, and now you know why I can't go down underneath the water. Or down deep into anyone else's life. I never told anyone before, and I won't ever again. You would think I would have moved to a desert. I can't even if I wanted to. I have to stay fascinated by water, but I can only stand to look at the waves.

After a while, I noticed there was a Bell Curve in every wave. There was a curve and a swinging up into the air that was inevitable. And a sound. Like I imagined a kiss might sound. Fairy tales spoke of mermaid lore, but now I understood it was a Brown noise.

I have to keep going to the water because I am stuck with the terror of dreaming of being under the water with Ernest's grinning face frozen in front of me almost every night.

The date of annual snow melt is of great interest as a potential indicator of climate change.

Chapter Seventeen

The Three Magi

Andy

One day I got a note. I was to call Map Girl. I handed the note to Bud. It read "Andy. Call me at two o'clock today. Map Girl."

I shuddered.

"I wonder if it's some more psychic stuff we have to do."

"You didn't do anything last time. I did." Bud protested.

"Uh huh," I said, and walked away.

Bud called after me. "Andy! Stop thinking so much and just call Map Girl. It's simple. Just keep it that way."

I answered the phone at two o'clock. Map Girl's voice came on. I could tell she was in her psychic mode because she was intoning her words like a fortune teller.

"Andy?"

"Yes."

"It's Miss Emma's turn. She's coming to the monastery. When she gets there, do everything she tells you to do, exactly like she tells you, and don't ask any questions. And wear blue every day. Without fail, always wear blue. Jeans, shirts, socks, underwear, shoes. Everything blue. Do you understand? "

"No, but I'll do it."

"I'm coming with her," Map Girl said.

I hung up the phone and turned away. Oh my God! Here we go again!

Bud Spinner

I snapped at Andy after he told us his news.

"Ben is journaling. You're fishing. I've found old engines to work on. What the hell more could they want from us?"

Ben and Andy just blinked at me and shrugged. Three fearful old fools. Three terrified old trembling Toms. Three old unexpected undertakers. It wasn't just us anymore. We weren't alone in this. Other people were starting to cling to us like burrs. It was clear that we were affecting lives. They'd been calling us "The Three Magi" ever since we stopped at the store. None of us knew why. We weren't stupid men. Just men who didn't want to make ripples in this old damned world. We did not need to or want to be responsible for any other human beings.

"Should we pack up and leave? We could be gone in a few minutes." I threw the question at them. Andy and Ben blinked again. I stood my ground and waited while they thought it over.

"Maybe we should... Okay... Let's go," Ben said.

"When are they getting here, Andy?"

"They didn't say, but it's at least a three day drive from the store to here."

"Well, we got some time then," Andy said. "I'm going fishing and eat some more potato chips."

Potato chips were Andy's favorite comfort food these days, next to fried pineapple pies.

"Want to eat dinner with the Brothers?" Ben asked.

Ben once told us that his hero worship of Superman as a child transformed him into the no frills steak and potato man he was today.

"They are having Salisbury steak tonight. We won't say a word about any of this to the Brothers. They may be in cahoots with them."

He shrugged.

"There isn't a damn thing we can do about it now anyway."

Map Girl and Miss Emma's Plans

Emma already knew the way I was. She'd known me too long. When I showed up at the ranch in a cloud of dust, she didn't seem too surprised.

"You're always welcome here," she greeted me.

"Come in and sit down, Mama. You look... good."

I knew she'd meant to say flustered but changed her mind and reworded her greeting. I sat down and waited while Emma sent Hilda to the kitchen for raspberry herb tea and small pastries. Emma sat down across from me and watched me with her steady, warm, dark velvet eyes and waited. I noticed a few threads of gray in her hair. They were becoming to her. After all, we were both grandmothers now.

I wrung my hands together and blurted out, "They're planning on leaving! We have to hurry!"

"Who's leaving?"

"The Three Magi!"

She knew who I meant.

"They are leaving the monastery?"

"Yes! And you must pack fast and bring your paints and canvas so you can paint the picture for Andy. It's time and he needs it. And you're supposed to do it!"

The words rushed out of me. I jumped up and paced the floor. I believe that beauty lubricates the soul like the oil that keeps the Merc' running smooth. Beauty was all around me in this room, but I had no time right now to admire it or let it soothe me.

"Well, I can't go right now."

"What?"

"When did you tell them we would be there?"

"I didn't."

"Well, why don't we call the monastery, and have the Brothers take a message to them right away saying that we will be there in two weeks. That I have a show to finish first."

She smiled at me.

"They don't have to know we're leaving day after tomorrow and bringing William with us. He gets here tomorrow. How about doing that?"

She shrugged and said calmly, "They may leave anyway."

We made the call, and then sat back down to tea. All of a sudden, I was relaxed and hungry. The tea and food was delicious. When we were done, Emma said, "Okay. Now tell me more of what it is you want me to do."

"Well, it's for Andy. The painting you're going to do. Just like you did before, when you painted in that big, sun filled room in the house you stayed in at the monastery."

I could see the room, though I'd never been there.

"I know you don't know what to do, and I can't tell you much, but you will know when the time comes right. We'll both know more then, I hope," I said ruefully.

Emma watched me for awhile. Then she stood up.

"I trust you."

It was time for me to go. She was artistic royalty, and I was what I was. The paintings she did and brought back from her last trip to the monastery were being hailed as fresh and powerful. They sold for hundreds of thousands of dollars.

Here I was, asking this famous artist to travel over a thousand miles to do some kind of painting for Andy and I didn't know what the painting was supposed to be of. It was a good thing that we'd known each other for a long time and that we were grandmothers together.

Emma, William, and I left for the monastery in a van filled with paints, canvases, and other things we were guessing we might need. We left the morning after he got to the ranch. We took turns driving and arrived at the monastery early on the third morning. The Brothers had our living quarters ready. We got the keys and quickly moved Emma into the same big house again and William the Dude and me into smaller houses just before seven in the morning. Then we penned a note and asked one of the Brothers to put it on the Three Magi's cabin door for us. All we could now do was wait.

Andy showed up at ten o'clock on the dot. Emma looked pale and exhausted from the tension of waiting. I watched her pull herself up into the regal soul she was as Andy stepped through the doorway, diffident and cautious.

He had done as I asked. He was completely dressed in shades of blue. Blue jeans, socks, shirt, even shoes. Dyed tennis shoes. When I told Emma what it was she needed to paint, she frowned and snapped at me.

"I don't usually paint those sorts of things."

I waited until she became unsurprised. Finally she sighed and said, "Okay. I'll give it a try."

"Get out," Emma ordered me and William. We heard her say to Andy.

"I'm to do a painting for you. So, I am going to paint, and you are to sit right here. No questions, understand? "

She led him to a chair by the window. The chair faced the outdoors.

Andrew Noble's Portrait

Miss Emma made me sit in a chair by the window. It took a lot of arguing with Ben and Bud before I was able to make the ten o'clock appointment. They were ready to leave, but Miss Emma won out. I stared out the window. The gardens and trees were filled with gold light and blue winds. Miss Emma had me looking away from the painting. But she sometimes came to the chair where I was sitting and paced around it, staring at me, searching something out with her sharp eyes. A couple of hours passed before Miss Emma covered the canvas so I couldn't see it and spoke to me.

"Come back tomorrow morning at seven o'clock."

"Okay."

I went back to the cabin, but it was empty. I was expecting Ben and Bud to be waiting to argue with me about posing for Miss Emma. They'd already asked me if I thought I was cute. I had no answers. No more than I ever did, so I got in my lifejacket and took the boat and my camera out on the lake. Someday I hoped to find the elusive something I was looking for and maybe get a picture of it. If I ever found it, I could rest easy again for the first time since I was a kid. But the something was associated with water, so it was not an easy task for me to search for it.

Sometimes I dreamed of what it would be like to not have this fearful, unknown obsession, this absolute need to hang around water searching for something deep within its depths, while not being able to get in the water. I was a dry docker, that's for sure, but I couldn't stay there.

The rest of the day went by as usual. Ben and Bud didn't mention anything about the painting process or leaving. We ate dinner with Map Girl and William the Dude. Nobody mentioned the painting.

I reported in at seven the next morning. Miss Emma sat me in the chair by the window again. I watched the sun come up the rest of the way. I could tell Miss Emma was frustrated with the painting. She paced around me and frowned and sighed. At eight thirty, she ordered me to leave.

"Be back at seven tomorrow morning."

I nodded and took off, glad to be gone. I didn't even try to glance at the covered canvas she stood in front of. I didn't give a damn what it looked like. I just wanted this ordeal to be over with.

The next day went the same. I dressed in all blue everything, including my underwear, just in case Miss Emma had X-ray vision of some kind. There was a lot going on here I didn't understand, and I intended to be as prepared as I could be for any event. At eight thirty, she told me to come back just before dawn the next morning.

That day, Map Girl and William took us on a long ride up into the National Park bordering the monastery. We visited a couple tourist towns and ate at a German restaurant. We wandered along a small river. In another little town, we discovered a vintage car dealer and looked over his cars. We got back just before dinner time, so William and Map Girl ate dinner with us at the cabin. Miss Emma's absence and the painting were not mentioned.

The next morning, I got up in the early dark, dressed in blue, and walked to Miss Emma's studio. The air was fresh and clean with an early breeze tangoing through the treetops. The studio was dark. A note was taped on the door.

"Go on in. Turn on the lights and look at your painting. I'll arrive soon."

It was signed, "Emma."

I turned the doorknob, went inside, flipped on the light switch. The smell of fresh paint lingered in the air. The walls of Miss Emma's paint studio were draped in all kinds of textures and shades of blue cloth. The large canvas was covered with a white cloth. The chair I set in by the window had been moved to the middle of the room to face the canvas. I wandered toward the canvas, taking my time. Finally, I reached up and pulled the cloth forward real easy. It slid to the floor.

A mermaid stared out at me from the canvas. She was under water, and she was looking at me. She wore a curious look on her face, as if she wanted to ask me many questions about the dry world I lived in. I stepped back until I fell into the chair. I knew I was looking at the most beautiful being I would ever see in my life.

The mermaid's hair was long and waving like water waves. She was young, like I once was. She looked just as surprised to see me as I was to see her. I gasped, and my breathing changed. Forever. I knew it was going to be forever, because she was here now.

All of a sudden, I felt like I was underwater with her. Fear instantly filled me. I looked around for Ernest, but I couldn't see him. He wasn't there. The mermaid was. I looked for the horror of seeing Ernest again under the water until I lost count. But every time I went under, the mermaid was there instead. She changed each time I met her under the water. Sometimes she smiled and sometimes she just looked at me.

After what seemed like an eternity, I jumped up, ran to the canvas, grabbed both sides of it and hung on to it until my breathing calmed down. Then I put my face to her face. She was older than I will ever be, and younger than I ever was. She held the health and beauty of the Dark and the Light in her face.

"I love you," I said. Startled by my own words, I looked around. The room was empty. Thank God no one heard what I just said! I'd never said those words out loud to anyone, ever before. I'd never thought them either.

I checked my breathing. It seemed to be just fine, only deeper and more stately. I touched the Mermaid's forehead with mine and put our hands together. After awhile, when I could stand leaving her, I scooted the chair about six feet back from her, sat down in it and watched her. I don't know how much time passed before I heard the sound of Miss Emma's shoes moving quietly into the room.

"We're going to the ocean. Now!"

She announced this in a firm tone of voice. I remembered that the monastery was located only a couple hundred miles or so from the ocean. I'd never seen the ocean. I bet that Ben and Bud hadn't either.

I shivered in stark fear. This was going to be bad for my nerves. But I was going to do it anyway. It was going to be all the way or nothing. Besides, Mermaid Girl had never seen the ocean either. I got up and went to the canvas and took it off the stand.

"Mermaid Girl goes too," I said.

"Of course she does." Miss Emma smiled.

I carried Mermaid Girl out to the waiting van.

"Oh my God! she's beautiful!"

Map Girl gasped in awe as I proudly stood Mermaid Girl against the van for them to marvel at. I had just named her!

"We have fasteners and protectors for the canvas inside the van on the left. She should fit nicely in there," Miss Emma said.

*

We climbed out of the van at the beach and Map Girl said, "We have beach clothes for you."

"Oh no!" Ben, Bud, and I protested. They were doing this to us because of the clothes we had worn to the store when we were so nervous and fear filled. Dismally, we eyed William the Dude, who stood waiting with a stack of brightly colored clothes in his hands.

"Well, we are at the ocean," Bud finally conceded.

William the Dude handed us the stack of clothes and grinned.

"Over there." He pointed at a row of small beach houses. "Just find an empty one to change in."

We looked William the Dude up and down. He wore a violently colored tropical shirt, ragged edged blue jean cut offs, and flip flops.

"Do you have flip flops for us, too?"

How did he know we wouldn't do it for the women?

So, Mermaid Girl and I went to the ocean together for the first time. We were overwhelmed and fearful at first, then blissfully awed by the water. Later Bud and Ben and I strolled along the shore and stared at the ocean and the sky while the wind and waves worked us over. Alternating between fear and wonder, we were like light bulbs being turned on and off. Map Girl ran up and down the beach, then linked arms with us.

"William the Dude is a practicing Dude-ist, did you know that?" she shouted over the wind.

"He's a what?"

"A practicing Dude-ist."

"You mean a practicing Buddhist?"

"No."

She laughed.

"He's a Dude-ist. He practices Dudeism. He's been ordained as a priest in Dude-ism. He's a Dudeist Priest. It's the most easy-going religion in the world. The guys that join it are dangerously full of it. You should ask him about it."

She skipped away. Then she stopped and looked back at us over her shoulder.

"Now," she ordered.

We stopped and looked at each other. Dude-ism sounded like a fearsome quackery of a religion.

"She was kidding, right?" Ben asked hopefully.

"I don't think so," Bud sighed.

We found William the Dude sprawled in a lawn chair by the van. He was drinking a Stroh's beer.

"Hey guys," he said. "Grab a beer."

We retrieved beers from the cooler by his feet and sat down in the empty lawn chairs by him. Nobody said anything for a long time. We just coped with the overwhelming environment around us as best we could. The birds hollered, the wind blew, the ocean roared, the sun was too bright, and the sand was gritty and hot. The big commotion we'd landed in was terrifying, but we withstood it.

"Map Girl said you were involved in something called Dudeism?" Bud finally asked.

William the Dude gave a startled laugh.

"Yep. I guess so!"

"She said that you're a priest in it or something?" Ben added.

"A Dudeist priest?" William almost fell off the chair laughing. "Yep. I'm an ordained Dudeist Priest!"

He laughed some more.

"You guys want to join?"

"What are the requirements?" Ben asked.

"That your goal in life is to become easygoing!" He laughed again. "But somehow, I don't think that's going to happen," he said.

We looked at each other, puzzled. Why did Map Girl sent us to talk to William about such a ridiculous idea? William shrugged and finished his beer. We tipped ours up too. Maybe we would never know.

Snow melts the fastest of all when the signs of a new spring season begin.

Chapter Eighteen

The Boy

Ben, Andy, and me watched in shock from the front porch of the cabin as the dark haired boy rode past on his bicycle. We'd settled in here, guaranteed that we would never be bothered by women or kids. Time was different here, so we sort of lazed through it like cats that finally found a safe hiding place to spend their time napping and eating. We never thought about anyone else disturbing our little corner of the world.

The boy risked a fast glance at us, but he didn't smile or linger with his gaze or his bicycle. He pushed his bicycle into high gear and pedaled past us as fast as he could. We were embarrassed at being caught staring at another person regardless of their age.

We looked at each other consideringly. Well, maybe he wouldn't pass this way again. Or maybe he was leaving.

"I never learned to ride a bicycle," I stated ruefully.

"Neither did I," Ben said.

"Me neither," Andy said.

We shrugged at each other's failure and let it go. The next day, while we were strolling down the dirt road toward the auto repair shop, the boy raced past us on his old beat up bicycle. It was much too big for him.

We turned as one and looked at the plants and trees, our backs to him, as he pedaled past us on his bicycle, keeping as far away from us as he could. Then we turned and watched him as he disappeared rapidly into the distance. Andy said what we were thinking.

"He acts as scared of us as we are of him."

We snickered chastely and then fell solemn. That was too bad. Life had chased us down until we landed here for a breather. We wondered what in life chased that boy down to this place.

A few days went by. The boy rode up and down the road in front of the cabin. We got used to seeing him and figured out he lived past us. We went for a stroll out of curiosity and saw his bicycle leaned up against the porch of the little white house just around a bend in the dusty road. There was a second bicycle beside of his. They were both old and looked like some of the bicycles the brothers rode.

We quickly turned around and headed back to the cabin. Being snoopers was a very delicate and uncomfortable role for us, as we were usually on the other side of the fence, busy being snooped upon. The boy looked to be about eight. He rode up and down the road, ignoring us, keeping his distance and speeding up when he saw us. We studied it out. At last Andy stated.

"The problem is, that bicycle is too big for that boy."

Ben said, "Yes."

We went to find Brother Tom.

"There you are!" he boomed at us as he led the way to the auto shop. Inside of one of the bays stood an old blue Chevy pickup. We stopped and studied it.

"Boys, it needs your help. The Brothers here can't figure out the carburetor system on it and a couple of other things."

We forgot our questions and moved as one over to the 1951 Chevy pickup and started looking it over. Ben was in the passenger side, Andy was under the back frame, and I had my head stuck under the hood when the boy rolled up on his bicycle.

"Hello Rayfield!" Brother Tom boomed at him. The boy flinched a little but stood his ground.

So the boy's name was Rayfield. An odd name.

"My back tire is almost flat. How do I fix it?" the boy asked in a voice filled with bravado. He looked around at all the men in the garage, ready to bolt. We all quieted down and moved easy and stayed right where we were while Brother Tom brought out an air pump and a patch kit. He helped the boy patch the tire and air it up while the boy kept one eye on us like a skittish colt would.

The boy looked up, met my glance and held it for a moment. I was startled, for he looked just like Miss Emma. After the boy left, we put down our tools and gathered around Brother Tom, obviously waiting for an explanation. Brother Tom hummed and rocked back and forth on his heels; a habit he had. He wouldn't volunteer any information. To break the standoff, I stated the fact.

"Rayfield looks just like Miss Emma."

Brother Tom looked crestfallen. He sighed and looked around, making sure nobody else was in hearing range.

"It's all a secret, okay? The kind you keep for someone to protect them? The kind of secret I know you fellas wouldn't have any trouble keeping, right?"

"We are not little kids in a secret club," Ben stated.

"We are already keeping secrets for some folks." Andy stated this in a matter of fact voice.

We waited while Brother Tom took a large white handkerchief out of his pocket and wiped his face off. He took his time. We knew he was buying time to think over what he would tell us. But we were not bullies, and he was too astoundingly large to ever be bullied, so we waited it out.

"Let's say that, hypothetically only you understand, that Miss Emma's son, who hypothetically might be married to Map Girl's daughter, might have hypothetically jumped the fence, and might have hypothetically had a son from it that nobody knew about until a week or so ago, and maybe Miss Emma and William the Dude don't want Map Girl to find out yet, and sent them to hide out here because the mother was beat up by someone who is dangerous and after her and Rayfield, and they need a safe place to hide."

He poured the whole statement out in one long breath from his barrel chest. We squinted at him. A long silence went on while we mulled his words over.

"How are you protecting them?" Andy finally asked.

Brother Tom waved his arms expansively in all directions.

"We have the usual security. The gates will stay closed and a guard will be posted when they are open. We have a couple of other things too. We can keep them safe here."

We turned and walked away, throwing a few words back at him.

"We are not blabbermouths. Never were," Andy said.

"Except for Ben when he is being painted," I added.

"He's a regular babbling brook then."

Brother Tom looked puzzled.

"We need to think about this, that's all. You can trust us," Ben added.

"Shut up, Ben," Andy said.

"You're turning into a regular blabbermouth again."

Ben ignored Andy.

"We'll get back to you later Brother Tom."

We walked back to the cabin, stunned into silence. We retrieved cold beers from the refrigerator and settled ourselves in chairs out on the back deck overlooking the lake.

"So the boy, Rayfield, I mean, and the mother are scared to death of people. That's what it looks like to me," I said.

"Me too," Ben added.

"I agree," Andy stated, as though he was judge sitting on a bench somewhere.

Whew! We all blew out our breaths together. Mean, jacked up life had found us again through a boy like we once were. Now what? We didn't have any answers. That was why we landed here to begin with.

Inevitably, our thoughts turned to being boys. We never got to be boys who played. We never learned the things boys usually learned to do. We couldn't ride bicycles or shoot bows and arrows or guns. We never chewed tobacco, or shot off fireworks, or built bonfires, or stayed up all night talking. We never got D.A. haircuts, combed our hair up into pompadours, or used Brylcreem as teenagers. We never owned ant farms or chewed Blackjack chewing gum, or wore letter sweaters, or sported sideburns. Instead, we stayed old and cautious and fearful, with neat butch haircuts and plaid shirts.

After a while, Andy said, "I wonder if Brother Tom has any extra old bicycles laying around?"

After a minute Ben answered. "No. That's not the way to do it. He'd know our business if we did it that way. We need to go to town and get new ones."

"How do we know what to get?" I asked.

"I don't know the first thing about bicycles."

"Well, we might get some darts and bows and arrows and maybe a pup tent too?"

We looked at each other with shining eyes. Maybe, just maybe, we could regain some of our lost boyhoods. A little piece of it, maybe just a sliver, but something.

Who knew what that kind of quest would do for our dormant, never used wondrous charm and personalities? We couldn't be boy scouts or anything like that, but there were unknown things to be learned, and kites we might just get to fly. We hoped Ben Franklin wouldn't be the only man who could have boyish fun with dignity after he became a man. He'd discovering electricity as his excuse for kite flying, so maybe we could disguise our play, too.

We looked through the phone book and decided to drive to a big sporting goods store located about sixty miles away. That way, just in case, word wouldn't get back to anybody about us three old fools who didn't know a damn thing about the life of a playful, happy boy. We would be embarrassed, but we probably wouldn't need to go that far away again. Only once.

We borrowed a truck from the monastery's auto shop and set out. It took awhile. When we got to the store, the clerks thought we were nuts when we asked to see the plainest bicycles they had. We were looking for the kind of bicycles we remembered from back when we were kids.

Finally, a tall, middle-aged man came out to help us. He hitched up his tan pants by his belt over his belly and gave us a wide, toothy smile. His eyes were the same blue as the oceans on our maps. His hair was thin and sandy and he leaned a lot toward stocky. The fragrance of peppermint rolled over us when he spoke.

"My name is Chandler Ames. How can I help you?"

"We want bicycles."

"Well, that shouldn't be a problem."

He shrugged heartily.

"Easy as water rolling off of a duck's back."

He led us to three old style Schwinn men's bicycles in green, red, and blue. They had pedal brakes, wide seats, and no wires or other contraptions on them.

"This what you're looking for?"

"Ah... Are there any instruction manuals on how to ride them?" I asked carefully, waiting for his reaction. He did a double take, walked up and down a couple of times in front of us with his hands behind his back, looking us over without a word.

Finally he said, "Ah... I think you're going to need some accessories."

He sold us long sleeved sweaters called trainers, long sleeved fitted sweaters called base layers, jerseys, and cycling shorts. He sold us wool arm warmers, knee warmers, caps and helmets. "Wear this stuff until you learn to ride real well. It will protect you when you fall."

He amended his words.

"I mean, if you fall. Then you can coordinate your colors like a cycling team does."

"There are cycling teams?" Ben asked. We looked at each other.

"Yes. There are many of them."

"You need patches and repair kits. too."

These bicycles might need more work to keep running than a damn truck!

"Make sure there are no cars around when you are learning. The bikes are the right size for you. Stand to the right of the bike when you get on. Hold both handlebars and swing your leg over. Walk the bike at first. Look ahead, not down at your feet."

He boomed instructions at us, but we'd had enough. We moved on to tents. We bought three pup tents, darts and a target, and bows and arrows and the bicycles and the other bicycle stuff, loaded it all into the back of the truck and headed back to the cabin. We wanted to start small. We unloaded our goods and took the truck back to the auto shop.

People exploit big hearted people, and we were. Big hearted. So we hid it. People exploit dumb people, and right now we were dumb about these things, but we didn't want to hide from the boy. Just from everyone else.

The next morning, we ate a hearty breakfast, the breakfast of three condemned men before we dressed in our new neon colored gear and solemnly walked our new bicycles out to the road to commence. Ben's bicycle was blue. Mine was green. Andy's was red. We didn't have any zest to offer. Just the long ago remembered fears of a lonely, bikeless childhood. We stood frozen beside the thin, dusty, winding little road, helmets on, dressed in too small wool sweaters with colorful fluorescent logos announcing different mountain tops on them and black tights, waiting for something to free us into the next step.

None of us had an ounce of intellectual poise left. Our joint terror of being conspicuous was gone. We'd lost it somewhere along the line. Now we were just shipwrecked, wanting to be, bicyclists. We stood frozen in a storm of violent agitation until we were interrupted by the sound of an engine. The old blue truck came slowly into view. As it got closer, we could see a small woman driving it. Beside her sat the boy we wanted to impress.

We sighed collectively, heavy with our failure, and stared down at the ground, waiting for them to pass. Three red faced old men in tight clothes. We hoped they would pass fast and not notice us too much.

But the truck stopped just past us. We heard the boy and the woman arguing about us.

"But Brother Tom said they were okay!" the boy said.

"Well, that's not good enough," the woman answered.

"But..."

"That's just men agreeing to hide each other's ways," she added. "Men are all bad. That's why we are here, hiding out from them."

"I thought we were just hiding out from Wade," the boy said.

"Men are all no good in the end!" the woman shouted at the boy.

By this time, we were looking up and straight at them. Figuratively, we took our fingers out of our ears and listened to the call of the good, wild man whose females had stolen their soul's best with hateful words down through time. We knew this bad thing was happening to the boy too. He was wilting like a little green stalk of celery on a hot day over one bad man. Her words lashed out and stripped all males within the area of their cojones. I wondered how Brother Tom fared with her. For an instant, I felt pity for him.

She only stopped because she wanted to verbally whip some men's asses, not for the boy. And we were too old to do anything about it, and she was in the old blue truck, and it was running. A fast getaway for her.

I got angry. Then I started feeling something unfamiliar to me. Tears started running down my face as I stared at her. I heard Ben sob next to me.

Andy was sniffling. We were too young emotionally right then to be ashamed of our crying. We were just boys with hopes of redeeming something from long ago, a precious something we had not dared dream of before. Those hopes were dashed to the ground by this mean woman's bitter words. She had taken away our possibilities of regaining a piece of joyful boyhood. We would never get it back.

"Oh my God! They are crying!"

She didn't know whether to laugh at us, or to be ashamed. Horror filled her shrill voice.

"Yeah, Mom. You did it again!" the boy shouted.

Anger slowly stopped my tears and overcame my terror. I found myself straddling the bicycle. I glanced over at Ben and Andy. Their grim looks told me they had reached the same place. They straddled their bikes, and we paddled along slow with our feet, like Chandler Ames told us to do. We were going to listen to him, not to her. Chandler Ames became Our Father Who Art. Loudly I recited what he told us to do.

"Make sure there are no cars around when you are learning. The bicycles are the right size for you. Stand to the right of the bike when you get on. Hold both handlebars and swing your leg over. Walk the bike at first. Look ahead, not down at your feet. When you start to use the pedals, straddle the bike and use one foot to start the pedal going forward. Set it at two o'clock. The clothes will help cushion your falls. Keep trying. Keep going forward. It will be easy in no time."

I finished the litany and started over. By then we were out of earshot of her voice. On bicycles, no less.

We stopped and looked at each other. We heard the truck move on. Then we moved on, padding our feet faster. When we stopped for a breath, Andy muttered.

"She's got a spiritual malaise, just like that damn town we lived in. It spread a daily fog of it everywhere. God help that boy."

He shook his head. We knew exactly what he meant. The boy's mother was stuck in seeing all men as bad. Until she learned that some were bad and some were good, she would live under that umbrella of hate, never seeing the sunshine good men provided every day on this planet.

Hate. It was a powerful thing. We none said the obvious. That same hate kept us from being light hearted boys and frisky young men. That hate of different kinds and sometimes it didn't take much, had stolen those years from us. That, and our constant introversion and fear.

"Let's move on," Ben said solemnly. "If we do, we can possibly overcome it. I won't give it a name."

We padded on a little further until we reached the incline in the road. All of a sudden it looked steep as hell.

"You go first, Bud," Andy said with a grin.

"Your turn next, Ben."

"Why do you get to go last?" Ben asked Andy.

"Because I have to get off my bike and give you guys a push."

Ben and I pondered this idea while Andy waited.

"Okay."

Andy gave me a push and I lifted my feet and wobbled down the hill. At the bottom, I managed to pedal a little further.

"Come on you guys!" I shouted.

Andy pushed Ben and got on his own bike and rode down the incline. Then we pushed our bikes back up the hill and did it again. Each time we reached the bottom, we used our pedals to go a little further. We wobbled along the dirt road, developing motor skills we'd never used before. After awhile, we got tired and went home, wobbling along on our bikes, sweaty and grinning with our accomplishment like the schoolboys we'd watched from afar back in our boyhood days. So this was what it was like!

Yeah, we had fallen down a couple of times, but the clothes Chandler Ames advised us to wear protected us. We were beginning to understand more of what a good father did. He provided protection, but also the courage to continue, and buffers to get through the school of hard knocks on the way. That's what boys who had good fathers knew. And I guessed that there were roving bands of cyclists everywhere that knew this amazing thing too.

Something was breaking loose in us. Something hard and cavernous was giving way. It was collapsing, allowing us to at last build something new. Whatever it was, was becoming last Wednesday's ashes, releasing us into a new time and magical place where old men could reclaim at least a part of their boyhood.

We were exhausted. There was a heightened awareness of our surroundings we'd never had before. Being this sensitized made us almost sick, so we hurried into the cabin, locked the door and collapsed on our beds. But that didn't work. The process was inexorable. It gripped us by the balls so to speak. We got back up and wandered around, muttering and sighing. We were who we were.

Somberly, we went back outside and straddled the bikes again. We rode up and down the road in front of the cabin, learning balance and speed and how to stop. As soon as we started again, we regained the intense, newly discovered feeling of youth and freedom. We grinned at each other. It was as much as we could do. Ben let out a hesitant yelp at one point.

"Yahoo!"

The old blue truck went back and forth a couple of times, but we vigorously ignored it. Finally we went back to the cabin again, this time because we were tired. Riding a bicycle was work. Good work, but still work. We fired up the grill on the back deck. Andy grilled steaks and Ben broke out a special bottle of wine he was saving for a special occasion. Me, I was the potatoes and plates and everything else man. Later, we all took hot showers and hobbled off to bed with tubes of liniment.

Three days later, with Ben's chain loose and a flat tire on Andy's bike, we decided it was time to go back to the sporting goods store and consult with Chandler Ames again. We needed our bikes repaired, and the thing none of us admitted was that we needed another Good Father fix if we were to carry on.

We borrowed the truck again and set out. The clerk remembered us. As soon as he saw us, he rushed to the back of the store and pounded on Chandler Ames office door. Out popped Chandler Ames.

"Calm down!" he boomed at the clerk. Then he saw us, and his eyes widened for a moment. We waited while he sent the young man back to sorting sports socks near the checkout counter. Then he hitched up his wide tan pants, turned to us, and smiled his big toothy smile at us again. We heaved a collective sigh of relief. Ben frowned and stepped forward.

"My chain came off."

Andy stepped forward.

"I got a flat rear tire."

Chandler studied us.

"Hmmm...."

We watched the wheels turning again as he studied us.

"Well boys," he drawled, "I'm glad you came back to see me."

He looked around.

"I meant us."

He winked at us and rubbed his hands together briskly. I liked the dry rubbing sound it made and noticed that his light colored eyebrows were bushy.

"Where are the bicycles?"

"Out in the truck," Andy answered.

He followed us outside and stopped and sniffed the air appreciatively.

"There's nothing like fresh air. I used to be a Bobcat Scout Leader, and we camped in every forest in the national park and climbed every mountain close to here. I liked to go up to Mount Rainier the best.”

He looked at the ground, cleared his throat and changed the subject. We studied the possibilities his words contained while he looked over the bicycles in the back of the truck. The huge, weary circle of life we had lived came to a stop with his next words.

“Well boys, take them out and let’s see what we can do to fix them.”

People make their own homes. They go from the womb to a cradle of some sort and then a crib and then a bed. All in a house with a mother and father, usually. We knew instinctively that Our Father Chandler of the Bicycle Prayers disguised as instructions, had suffered something terrible. And we also knew unerringly that he had grown up with a good mother and father. So what could be wrong?

We waited, but he said no more about his past. He was a vast talker, but not a B-esser. His words poured out, sounding like spheres, each one complete and round and oddly comforting, like bubbles popping in a bubble bath.

“We got a little shop out back, boys. Let’s take them out there. We got to go through the store to get there, though.”

We followed his broad back. It looked like it could hold up the world with no trouble. When things change, one simply has to adapt. We were in a stage of convalescing, and he was the doctor, though he didn’t know it, and we had no way of knowing if he was qualified for the job yet. Especially since we didn’t know what the job was.

"Hey, Bob! You got a minute? These boys need some help with their bicycles."

He turned to us and explained.

"Bob here is our bike man. One of the best."

We followed them through the store. Bob fixed our bicycles and explained the processes to us while Chandler Ames rocked on his heels and hummed happily, his hands clasped behind his back. He sold us argyle socks and more repair tools for our bicycles.

"Well, you boys come back pretty soon," Chandler Ames said when we left. "Got some new stock coming in soon."

We knew he thought he was just being a salesman to three foolish old codgers. That was okay with us. He didn't know how much more he was becoming to us, at least until the process we were going through got finished. Neither did we. We went home satisfied. The next step had been taken in our journey.

*

One day Brother Tom came to see us. He came in and sat down and wiped his face with his large handkerchief, something we now knew he did when he was on a mission to accomplish something. We waited for what that might be.

"I heard you bought bicycles and are ah...progressing right along with them."

We nodded.

"I heard your bicycles are nice looking and new. I'm wondering where you got them."

We stared at him. We were not giving up Our Father Chandler Ames to him for any amount of Hail Mary's.

"Why?" I finally asked.

"Well, Rose wants to buy Rayfield a new bicycle for his birthday. Problem is, she doesn't want Rayfield or her to have to leave the monastery grounds, and I don't want her to either. Would you gentlemen consider procuring him a bicycle?"

Ben, Andy, and I looked at each other. So Rose and Rayfield were the mother and son Brother Tom had "hypothetically" told us about. That would make him Map Girl's grandson! That boy had hero's blood running in his veins, and one hell of a mean mother. How about that?

"Rose wants to give him a birthday party next Tuesday afternoon in the main room. Can you have his bicycle here by then? Do you need money?"

"Yes to the first question. No to the second one."

Brother Tom shook his head.

"Okay. I got to get back. See you later."

The delicate, dangerous daredevil matters of the human heart were coming into play, edging in on our lives, darkening them with unknown evils and passions. We couldn't stand it. It was as simple as that. We hastily piled into Ben's 51 Dodge Coronet Coupe and made the long drive back to the sporting goods store.

The clerk saw us and ran to get Chandler Ames.

"Back so soon, boys?"

He spoke in his usual jolly manner, strolling out of his office.

"What can I help you boys with?"

I nudged Ben forward since he was the blabbermouth of the bunch.

"Well, there is this mean woman who has a son who is turning nine next Tuesday, and we want you to have somebody deliver a new bicycle to his party Tuesday afternoon at two o'clock, so we don't have to go to it."

Ben looked at Andy and me. We nodded yes. We couldn't think of anything else to say.

Chandler Ames scratched his neck with his finger while he mulled Ben's statement over.

"Okay. Let's do this one step at a time," he said, rubbing his hands together. They made that dry sound I liked.

"What's the kid's name?"

"Rayfield."

"And this mean woman?"

"Rose."

"Okay. I'm going to assume that Rayfield is the usual size of a nine year old boy."

His voice shook and he stopped and took a deep breath.

"This is a little hard for me, boys, 'cause I lost my boy and his mother in a car accident three years ago. He was nine."

We were shocked and appalled. Our Father had been hurt badly. He had endured a Tragedy in his life.

"We'll leave."

"No. This is good for me. I need to do this. You Three Oddball Monk Men have brought this gift to me for some reason, so I will do it. That's all."

He had called us Three Oddball Monk Men. Map Girl had called us the Three Magi. What was it about us? We drank monastery beer and rode bicycles now. Maybe it was something to do with that. We picked out a red Schwinn bicycle for Ray and asked for all the bells and whistles to be added it to it.

"Here's a thought," Chandler Ames said. "Why don't I deliver it to the party myself? Where is it by the way?"

He sighed.

"Maybe it's time I seen another happy boy my son's age."

"Can you stand it?" Ben asked.

"I haven't been to church since it happened because my son's friends go there. This would be a start. Or maybe another stop. I might as well find out which. Where do I bring it to?"

"To the Brothers monastery."

We named the small town near the monastery. Chandler Ames laughed.

"I know right where it's at."

I said, "They have a lot of security so we will let them know you are coming. But you aren't to tell anyone anything about today or where you are going, because it could put Rayfield's and Rose's life in danger. She's been beat up, and they are hiding out. Someone dangerous is after her. This is a secret birthday party."

"Whew! Okay. I can do that."

He grinned at us.

"Boys, my life just got more exciting than it's been in a long time!"

We gave Chandler Ames our phone number, the monastery phone number and address and told him where our cabin was located. Then we rode back to the monastery and told Brother Tom that Chandler Ames would be delivering the bicycle and attending the birthday party on Tuesday. We didn't ask him for his okay. We told him. After we explained the circumstances to him, he was fine with it.

"If you three trust this guy, I guess I can too," he said. We didn't tell Brother Tom that Chandler Ames had become more than Our Father to us when he told us about his son. He had become Our Friend, too. We also didn't tell him that we didn't want to attend the birthday party for Rayfield, that we planned to show up and leave just as soon as we could.

"Wisdom is no longer being sought after in a desolate market where none come to buy." Ben muttered as we left.

"Something like that. I think that's by Blake."

Who the hell knew what that meant?

Two o'clock Tuesday came around. We dressed up and rode our bicycles to the main house. Some of the Brothers and Rose and Rayfield were standing around in the main room, talking quietly. Rose was still marbled with black and blue around her eyes. A few wrapped gifts lay on the table along with a very large cake and plates and forks. That was it. A very simple, and somehow very mournful gathering.

Only Rayfield's face betrayed his boyish excitement and hopes for his special day. He looked puzzled and almost sad in flashes, and I knew it was because there were no other children at his party.

Grownups can only do so much. They can't carry a child's excitement over very good, and then only in spurts if they remember how. And children always know when they are faking.

We stood around drinking punch for a few minutes. Beer wouldn't have been appropriate at a kid's birthday party. We felt sadder and sadder. The Brothers looked gloomy and martyred. Rayfield and Rose stood frozen with punch glasses in their hands, matching frozen smiles on their faces. What could we do? What kind of agony was this? This couldn't go on much longer or we would all freeze to death. Desperately we looked around for Brother Tom. He wasn't around.

All of a sudden, the double front doors burst open. In marched Chandler Ames, Brother Tom, and a whole bunch of boys singing Happy Birthday at the top of their lungs. The boys were around Rayfield's size, and they wore scout uniforms.

Chandler Ames led the way, guiding Ray's new red bicycle toward him. It had a giant red bow and canary yellow flames painted on the sides of it. It had a basket on it with flowers in it. Chandler Ames handed the bicycle over to Ray. Chandler Ames grabbed the flowers out of the basket, made a deep bow, and shoved them into Rose's unwilling hands. Then he turned to Brother Tom who was holding the largest box of chocolates I've ever seen, took it from him, grabbed the flowers back, laid them on top of the box, and shoved the whole thing into Rose's protesting arms.

The boys had just stopped singing when Chandler Ames bellowed at Rose, "Sweets for the Sweet!"

Everyone laughed in the silence, then started talking. The boys clustered around Rayfield and examined his new bike. The Brothers were visibly relieved and smiled at each other calmly. We watched Brother Tom say something to Chandler Ames, but Our Father wasn't listening. He was staring at Rose and she was staring back at him. We edged closer and heard her ask "Why did you do this? You don't know me."

"I did this in honor of my wife and son, whom I lost in an auto accident three years ago. She was lovely and he was a fine boy; your Rayfield's age. I bet you feel mean because of what life has handed you to deal with, and you got a bunch of hate and stuff going on, like hating men. Well, life could take you and your son out, like it did my wife and son at any instant, and I want you to know that I am a good guy, always have been, always will be. I'm proud of that and have no guilt about my life that I need to make up to you for. So don't charge me for causing any of your damage. The candy is between you and my sweet wife. The flowers are for your son's romps through the childhood I hope you will allow him to have in spite of your own problems."

His huge form swayed and hovered over little mean Rose gently, as his strong words found their way to her. He broke his eye contact with her and glanced at us.

"Time for more punch, boys?"

We knew when we weren't wanted. We moved away quickly. We left right after the cake was cut. Chandler Ames and Rose were still ignoring everyone else. They were staring at each other like two fascinated adolescents who had just encountered the hormones of the opposite sex for the first time. When that happens to people, they don't give a damn about their own miserable history. We had observed this phenomenon before.

We rushed out the door and got on our bicycles and pedaled toward the cabin. We jumped off of our bicycles and hurried into the cabin, locking the door behind us. Lord, what had we done? We had somehow brought together our Good, Kindly Our Father with the meanest mouthed woman around!

It was going to take hard liquor to handle this one! Ben already had the one bottle of Jim Beam we owned out. Andy was rummaging around for glasses. A great foreboding came over me. It suggested to me that Andy, Ben, and me would equally love and be exasperated by Chandler Ames in the future. But he would teach that mean woman to not mistake common cruelty for emotional kindness. Maybe that would be enough for the boy to be able to stand his life. Maybe Chandler Ames would become an Our Father to yet another lost boy, another boy whose father didn't want him.

Age didn't seem to make any difference in these matters, for we had become Chandler Ames lost boys in our own way, too. I liked what he said to Rose. Maybe my mother should have had those strong words said to her. Or my father. Chandler Ames was capable of being an Our Father to many, for he wasn't afraid of this world, and he was large hearted. It was plenty good enough.

The terror of the power we lost to choose what our lives might become belonged back in Ardenville, and it felt like it was being left behind where it belonged.

*

Autumn came, and the golden red dusk of our lives glowed with many new possibilities as we rode our bicycles. We got up early, ate cold biscuits and marmalade, and left the cabin dressed for the day in our riding clothes. We didn't know how long we would be gone, so we carried water jugs and more cold biscuits with us.

Ben was the biscuit maker and we kept him on the ball. Every evening as the autumn sun set, he pushed another pan of biscuits in the oven to bake. Andy buttered and jammed the biscuits when they came out of the oven. I did nothing. I couldn't. I couldn't provide food for myself, just water. Ben and Andy left me alone about it after they realized I was serious.

Our conscience was clear. We united in bike riding around the lake and all over the place. Our biggest goal was to someday have a barbeque contest with some prime athletes and win so we could say we beat real athletes at something. Gradually, as we gained more confidence, we began to ride some of the trails in the national forest behind the monastery.

We asked Brother Tom if it was okay to ride there, and he gave us the go ahead. Then he asked with a grin, "Want to know what's going on with Chandler Ames?"

"And Rose?"

We hadn't wondered. We knew Chandler Ames had taken over, so everything would turn out good because he was an Our Father man. He would be an Our Father man for the boy too. And the woman. We knew it. We had done our job, unknowingly and inadvertently. We hadn't seen any of them since then.

"Ain't asking, ain't begging," Andy said.

Brother Tom laughed, as though Andy was joking.

"Well, when William said you guys were the Three Magi, and to watch out for the gifts, God only knows what they might be, I thought he was just making a joke. But after watching the three of them together, I understand why he said that."

We looked at him, puzzled.

"Who?"

He laughed.

"You can't kid me. They see each other every day or talk on the phone. Rayfield and him spend time together. They are crazy about each other. Rose's meanness has fled. You knew Chandler Ames needed them just as much as they needed him. How did you plan that? Chandler's wife was beat down by a mean man before he taught her to love and trust him. They spent happy years together. A man who lost his wife and a son at the same ages as Rose and Rayfield are now."

Brother Tom shook his head slowly in wonder. So did we. We didn't say anything. We were too embarrassed. Brother Tom didn't know that we cried when Rose went after us. Better Chandler Ames than us trying to deal with that tartar! After a minute of too much emotional confusion and intensity filling the air, we turned and walked away.

"Boys, there is some crazy people giving us three ornery bastards credit for stuff we don't have a clue about! What do you think about it?" Ben looked at us.

"Not a damn thing!' Andy said testily.

"Let's ride!"

We hopped on our bikes and fled to the nearest path leading out of sight of the main building, where Brother Tom stood watching us.

As the red, orange, rust, and purple leaves on the trees hid us from Brother Tom, we became three carefree boys again. I wondered if there were angels whose careers were spent being Professional Surprisers. If there were, they sure had a lot of job security with us three.

Eliminated by loss at low elevations, snow can disappear altogether.

Chapter Nineteen

Mama

All of the Misfits are coming home for Christmas. In some ways I hope Christmas never comes because the urn with Cowboy Johnson's precious ashes will have to come out from under his cot and be shared. I don't want to share them. They're all I have left of his blood and bone to keep me company.

I'll never be lonely for the love of another man. I'll never look at a sunset or a homemade shower or an El Camino without thinking of him. He loved me well and far beyond the boundaries of hate and hurt we both overcame to be with each other. I know that now.

I don't know how I will be when Christmas comes. I may share his ashes with my beloved Misfits or I may try to talk them into letting me keep the urn under the cot a little longer. I know this much. I need them all to come home.

This year Miss Emma is bringing The Three Magi home from the monastery for Christmas. I don't know what to think of that, but I have to let her for she loved Cowboy Johnson too. I wish the Three Magi could have met him. He was cut from the same cloth as them. I am glad Bud brought me the new map. It was the message that told me that taking the road trip I am secretly planning is the right thing to do.

I feel restless in a new way, kind of like a tumbleweed must feel, all brown and edgy and prickly at unexpected times. As though I need to tumble or something, to get my balance back.

William is coming home early. He phoned and said he and Algestine, Timmon, and the two Mafia sisters would be staying out at the ranch with Emma. I wanted to cry, I was so disappointed.

"I need you to stay here at the store."

I held myself back from breaking into a wail. I waited through a long hesitation.

"How about we decide all that after we get there? I have to stay at Emma's for most of the time because she is involved in creating a trust fund for Celia, and we have to make decisions about the ranch, too."

He knew how to get to me. Celia was my weakness. Anything being done for her suited me just fine. Plus, I heard the edges of sadness in his voice. Sometimes I forgot how old he was, such a kind and gentle man, such a good friend! I wanted to weep but held it back.

"I love you William. Don't mind me. You do whatever you think is best. I trust you completely. You already know I am a little bit off of my rocker trying to get through these spaghetti days."

He chuckled.

"Thinking you're going it alone again, aren't you?"

I nodded, even though he couldn't see me, remembering when we first met at the store. I had seen him as a dusty old prospector the first couple times we met, but not for long. I had loved him from maybe twenty minutes on after our third meeting.

"Yes."

"Well, you're not."

"I guess you're right." I sighed heavily. I sounded theatrical, even to myself. I caught myself.

"Hector and Annie taking care of everything okay?"

"Yes," I answered.

Hector, one of the ranch hands, and his wife Annie, had taken over running the store and motel. We got off the phone, and I wandered out to the back porch and sat down. I never wanted to be far away from Cowboy Johnson's ashes. I got up and wandered into the back room. It was time to put the chicken on to roast so I would have something for dinner. I muttered the familiar litany to myself as I stood over the kitchen sink, fixing dinner for only me.

"Christmas time will come. I know it will. It won't be long now. Then they will be here with me.

Normaine will be home.

So will Eddy.

So will William the Dude.

And Timmon.

And my darling Geena.

And my sweet Celia.

And Ray.

And Algestine.

Maybe the three wise men.

And the Mafia sisters."

It came up on seven o'clock. The store was closed and locked up. Hector and Annie were gone. The front lights were out. I was alone. I ate some chicken, washed my plate, and stored the leftovers in the refrigerator. Then I slid the cardboard box out from under his cot and opened it again. I took out his journal and read in it like I did every night. A page at a time. The pages brought him back to me.

*

Cowboy Johnson's Journal

I discovered when I was a young man that I owned an old soul. I knew back then that I would always be an old man, so I avoided my absent, disinterested parents, and took full advantage of the finer learning opportunities afforded to my wealthy family. I became an educated, learned loner, and learned how to travel the world by myself. Proud and lonely, I was my father's second blood son. Perry, my older brother, the only other blood son, was always away somewhere. We were the only two children from father's bloodline. Perry was the closest thing I ever had to a friend until I met William at prep school and we quickly became friends.

Now, there was a thing that kept happening to me. I thought I didn't like girls. You see, my mother left me as a baby and moved to Europe. I was left to be raised by nannies and nurses. My father remarried twice. My two stepmothers didn't like me. The second one, Dawn, brought her two daughters and a young son into her marriage to my father. My two stepsisters, Valerie and Suzanna, resented their little brother, and said he hadn't belonged to their father. They called him a bastard behind Dawn's back.

My two stepmothers wore careful looks when I was around. They kept me at arm's length in a house

195

filled with silent pain and the shouts of the impatient rage my father lent to the slaps and names he called me and the rest of the family.

We were staying at our house in the Hamptons when it happened. Valerie and Suzanna took their brother out on the pond in a rowboat and he drowned. I believe they drowned him. I was walking the beach a few miles away, but they told Dawn and my father that I was in the boat and pushed him overboard.

I came home from my walk on the beach a while later and went in the back door. I heard voices and hurried to the front of the house. The police and ambulance and shocked neighbors were gathered there. Something was being loaded into the ambulance. My father rushed at me and shoved me back into the house. He propelled me swiftly through the house into the pantry off the kitchen.

"I know you did it, but we are never going to talk about it again. I've got Albert packing your things and you, young man are going away!"

"I was walking on the beach!" I protested. I figured they'd lied as usual, blaming something they did wrong on me again.

"Like hell you were!" He hissed at me; his face filled with loathing.

"Carl is dead! You satisfied?"

"What?" I shouted.

"No! I didn't do anything. They are lying!"

"It figures you would try to blame someone else! The police don't know, and never will. This is to be kept in our family because I don't want my son to rot in jail the rest of his life!"

"They must have done it!" I said.

He turned his back to me.

"Suzanna and Valerie said you would try to blame them. Stay here until Albert comes to get you. Don't talk about this. No one knows. Except us."

Back to school I went.

I was eleven years old. Something inside of me twisted and sickened with grief, and I never felt the same again. I was never that carefree boy again. I set out to slowly destroy myself.

I never told William I had been wrongly blamed for a murder. Desperate, sharp edges of rage and pain and fear became my devout companions. I was slowly dying from the poison of being accused of an evil I didn't do, a mother who neglected me, and a father who bore no faith in me.

One warm summer day, two years later, I was wandering along a cobbled street in Madrid, depressed, lonely, not watching where I was going. I was thinking about where I could find a bridge to jump off of and end it when a lovely girl with long, dark, curly hair swished past me and smiled. Her eyes were like dark almonds and bore that shape. Her chin was sharp and dimpled. Her smile showed her even, white teeth, and her red lips looked very soft. Her perfume lingered in the air. I stopped and stood in it and sniffed. I heard a laugh behind me. She came back and took me by my hand and led me away. A new place to go. I didn't have to die. I was saved. Carmella. She was my first lover, and she saved my life.

Through her, I discovered my great love of women. Women's love would warm me and keep me alive. Women sensed my love of them and loved me back. All ages and shades and heights and weights of women were attracted to me. When I went out, women came to me like flies to honey. I reveled in it. Through them, I learned there were all kinds of love women wanted and didn't want.

My education expanded steadily. The sharp edges of my pain were soothed away with soft, warm words and the touches and laughter of much lovemaking. I loved my sexual healing. It was a gift to me. All of them wanted to be heard and understood and loved.

I stayed away from women when William and I were together. I didn't need them then. He was important to me. He was my only close friend. We were together each year for the holidays and in the summer when school was out.

Both our parents were happy with our friendship. It let them off the hook. We roamed the world, avoiding our families, which they seemed to appreciate, carelessly spending from the deep wells of money we would inherit someday. It was a form of running away, and we both grew very adept at it.

After a few years, we became bored with our lifestyle. There must be something more. The women became more and more exotic, but the flames burned lower and lower. I needed to learn new things about love. We were running in a circle, never getting anywhere.

Perry kept in touch and told me how our father and Dawn and her two daughters were doing. He said they felt secure in their positions in our father's life, though he wouldn't bet the bank on the old man staying with Dawn forever because she treated him contemptibly. He was surprised at our father putting up with it.

With Perry's revelation, I realized instantly why they felt so secure, when our father was famous for his roving eye and womanizing ways. They were emotionally blackmailing him for what they said I did to Carl. He was paying for the murder he thought I committed. He believed his son killed his wife's son. That's what was keeping him in the marriage. That realization caused a fire to start deep in my belly. My gut twisted once again in remembrance and rage, like it did back the day Carlton was drowned. Our father hadn't spoken to me since he sent me hastily away on that calm, sunny day more than six years ago.

I wanted to shout the truth from the rooftops. But then, how would I prove my innocence? The papers reported Carl dying of an accidental drowning. The papers were full of Dawn, Suzanna, Valerie and my father's sad face as he shielded them from the press. The only mention of Perry and I was a one liner at the bottom of the stories saying we would join our loving family at the earliest possible moment.

I was so incensed, I thought I might die from the wrongs these women had perpetrated on my family. I walked the floor night and day, and quit eating. I drank and stayed bitter and turned mean. William asked me what was wrong, but I was in too deep of a hole to tell him what the trouble was.

I stayed drunk for months. William had patience and never left me. One night, after a particularly long binge of vodka and misery, William took me to the local hospital with alcohol poisoning. When I was well enough to leave, William took the situation in hand.

"Damn it, Avery! I'm not going to stand by and watch you destroy yourself over whatever the hell it is that ails you! I've had enough!"

After a minute he grinned.

"Let's go to India. I hear it's a place of enlightenment, and we both need that!"

We left for India. We met Krishnamurti there, and that meeting changed our lives. We were never the same again.

Krishnamurti asked us, "Do you want to do this? For there is no going back."

We dived in with both feet. My soul returned to me. The burning rage consuming me and destroying me gradually left. It took a few years, but my gut was no longer twisted. In its place was a new balance, a new calmness. I understood now that it was Karma working its force upon our lives. I came to believe that the life force runs the world and all that is in it. For awhile life was wonderful. We didn't know that we would hunger for our old habits and bitterly resist their loss. We didn't know that we would never become the scions of our wealthy families and continue their wrongful habits. Life had changed us forever.

But our families weren't through with us yet. And we couldn't fight back the way we used to before we went to India. But darkness has its own kingdom and powers. Many things change when the inevitable darkness descends. The elements change. Darkness has its own laws it lives under. And we both had to learn a funny thing. That darkness holds a gentle persuasion toward Goodness. That darkness can often repair what the Light of day cannot. There is a breakpoint in the Darkness. A place where I came to know inside myself that everything would work out all right.

One night, I was standing under a black sky filled with stars, looking up at them. After awhile, in the dark, weighted silence, I gradually became aware of knowing something that I never realized before. The new awareness settled into me gently. It walked in, searched out its proper place in my soul, sat down and rested there. Maybe it had bunions from walking so long, weary from searching for its place. It had been away a long time. That's when I went looking for my church.

*

I closed his journal and placed it carefully back in the box, put the lid on, and slid the box back under the cot. Then I put our song on the Victrola and pretended I was dancing with him. Once in awhile, when I got angry instead of being sentimental, I went out to Washman's Draw and shot the red cactus. I wasn't afraid to go out there by myself anymore. Cowboy Johnson kept his small snub nosed pistol in the glove box of the Merc'. He kept it there just in case there was ever any trouble.

Plugging God for taking Cowboy Johnson away from me was my first choice for a long time, but now I wasn't so sure. Now there were others to be considered. Dawn and Suzanna and Valerie for starters, bad people I met in his journal. People who murdered.

Bud Spinner and the other two wise men didn't nickname me Map Girl for nothing. They knew I could figure out things nobody else could. Like Mina, I instinctively knew I could use my Sight to take Cowboy Johnson's enemies down. Without a bullet fired, I could ruin their lives on Cowboy Johnson's behalf. I knew the power of the negative could harm even more through a person with the Sight, and I wanted every tool at my disposal to use when I dealt with Cowboy Johnson's Monsters.

Me. A naïve, silly woman with next to no looks, but a love for their rejected, blamed child that could rival the desert for the heat of my anger and emptiness. I owned a love that would fill all the space in this desert for the child they brutalized with merciless blame and neglect. A child they blamed for a murder they'd committed, leaving him helpless and running until he found the store, until it became an oasis where he hid from them and thrived because of us misfits.

I knew now that his elegant, learned, earned softness had beamed from his soul and attracted a Spirit Master who helped him survive. The beauty of his being was met and seen by his Master, and the gifts given to him. I loved a most sacred, beautiful soul.

In my life, I have been given both Bad and Good men to deal with. I ran from one and found shelter with another. My secret plans were coming into place. Meanwhile, the misfits were coming home for Christmas. I needed to prepare myself for that because it would mean that Cowboy Johnson and I wouldn't be alone anymore.

Year to year variability changes the picture of how much base snow is left each spring.

Chapter Twenty

My name is Andrew Noble, and I have fallen quietly into surrender. I have always been grouchy
Crotchety
Cross
Choleric
Crabby
Cranky
Obtuse
Irascible
and easily provoked.
I share those qualities with my friends Ben Bass and Bud Spinner.
The three of us are changing. It isn't changes that can be seen much on the outside. Unless you know us, you wouldn't notice that Ben's voice has deepened, and Bud's gestures aren't so sharp and precise anymore.
My life changed forever the day I met Mermaid Girl and we went to the beach together. Ernest left, never to return. It was finally time for me to learn to swim—metaphorically at least. Water carries memory, and mine was changed with the help of my new friends. With their gracious help, I broke a bad old pattern. A new world is opening itself up to me. When I go under the water now, not the real stuff I mean, but if I ever go under again, I know I will see Mermaid Girl's face instead of Ernest's. In fact, I

might someday become resolutely intrepid about the water. Dauntless in mid stream. Courageous when wet, a Wader along safe shores.

I needed to express my gratitude to Miss Emma for the painting of Mermaid Girl. I was changing for the better. I offered to pay her for Mermaid Girl, but she refused. The living room wall of the cabin had a picture window overlooking the lake. Ben, Bud and I positioned Mermaid Girl on the opposite living room wall so she would be looking out the picture window at the lake. I couldn't leave her in the light because she would fade. Miss Emma sent people to fix our lighting properly to protect her. After all, Mermaid Girl was a magnificent work of art in her own right.

Before William the Dude, Miss Emma, and Map Girl left, they extracted promises from the three of us to stay at the monastery until after Christmas, at least. We are traveling to the store to spend Christmas with them. They are our family now.

This summer, the dogged, dark introspection we three have carried all our lives began to slowly ebb away like waves washing a beach clean. Map Girl warned us that she would be clearing our lineages on the energy planes.

Summer passed. Our security chains stayed solid. Nothing happened to rattle them. No Dan Swain, no contact from relatives, nothing.

The three of us biked the monastery grounds, learning where things are located. The monastery borders a national forest. The grounds cover endless miles, including the lake our cabin is on, a dark green forest and a few other houses and buildings. All of them are hidden from each other's view.

Gardens and fields of crops grow for use in the brewery, barns, and kitchens. The barns hold livestock and a dairy in which they make butter and dairy products.

Day after day this summer, we familiarized ourselves with the monastery and the attitudes of the Brothers. We ate with them and drank beer with them. It helped us that there were hardly any strange people around. By that time, fall colors were in the trees. The air became crisp and clean, filled with pungent fall smells on the wind. The lake rippled with tiny white waves while Mermaid Girl watched from her safe place in the cabin.

By then, Bud was teaching the basics of mechanics to some of the Brothers. Ben was journaling and working in the kitchen and learning about herbs and food chemistry and engineering the development of new kitchen aids.

As for me, I stay on my knees in the vegetable garden in gratitude, and fish in the lake by the cabin with Mermaid Girl watching me through the window. We would never bloom into orange tiger lilies bordering hot summer fields or carry the purple knowledge of violets hiding in the shade. Those were lighter than we had ever been.

We owed an allegiance to our gravity, owed our respects to the peculiar shyness that once weighed heavier on us than lead. We owned stone faced patience. Masters of it. We were filled with gloomy rooms full of unfinished, boring and sad stories.

Between Ben and me, our families held a criminal psychopath, at least two schizophrenics, a mother who could bake the best yeast raised glazed sweet rolls, a father who was dogged and ornery and obtuse as an army tank, bossy sisters, hysterical liars, and the rest of the personalities and attitudes that rural America bred into its mainstream families. At least we never tried to drive tractors while under the influence.

Ben shattered early and decided that spaceship travel was safer than staying in his crazy home. That's where the science fiction came in and saved him. Couldn't blame him for that. Making a survival plan took intelligence, and he had that in spades.

Bud Spinner was an only child with a mother who ran away and didn't like him, and a sour puss father who died early.

Ben and me and Bud were all together in this. We didn't need anybody else. And it was good. We were now old things, a living library of fossilized old Dudeists, filled with untold stories and yens that would never be fulfilled. Yes, William the Dude and his congregation had converted us. The three of us put together sure make a hell of a team when it comes to dealing with life. Apart, I don't know what would have happened, but it wouldn't have been good.

Putting the Shadow down and running in fear from it didn't work. What we wanted to change in us needed to be treated with respect now. It was time to go into the living library that we were and find that section of divinity where our Shadow resided and show it our respect. It would tell us how. We could no longer treat it badly. It wasn't a boogeyman, just a section of our divinity that we needed to give recognition and respect to, or we would stay stuck.

We were to learn to treat what we thought of as the bad parts of ourselves with understanding and patience. We couldn't go the old route and try to kick its ass out or set conditions on our approval of it. It was Light hiding, assuming it was bad because we kept telling it that it was. It was time for the saboteur to lay down it's sword. The Shadow was the Survivor.

Ben Bass

Page 37 in my Starship Journal

We are looking forward to relaxing snowfalls this winter in our new home. Snow invites contemplation of our internal landscapes. Snow is drawn to the ways of the old. That's us! The moon and the stars are a part of our deeper feelings. They live within our bones, holding together the structure of the bonds formed during our creation way out there in the universe.

Snow creates negative spaces as it falls, and it takes the sharp edges away. Amen.

Snow fills in the empty places and covers the odd, treacherous, icy paths with solitary confinement. Amen.

Snow is organic and alive and is born in our universe of late and unhurried crystal emotions. Amen.

I hope it snows a lot this winter. We have snowmobiles and other equipment waiting for it. I can see more galaxies and planets and supernovas from here because it is darker and quieter than the little Podunk town we used to live in. I haven't told the guys, but I got a little bit of arthritis going on. I'm damned scared of getting old, but don't want not to either. What's the alternative? As long as I can still rev up a snowmobile, I'll be okay.

Bud Spinner

The first snowflakes started falling. The three of us sat on the back deck of the cabin and drank a beer in celebration. The snowflakes settled on us, and we looked at each other, understanding without words the benevolent benediction Nature was pouring over our Dark natures.

We were no longer invisible.

We were no longer young and sad and empty. For the first winter in our lives, we were not in our hometown when the snow started falling. If it turned out to be a blizzard coming in, it would be okay, for we had traveled long miles to get to this monastery with a brewery, a cozy cabin, and new, trustworthy, at least so far, friends.

I'm napping lately. Sweet, short sleeps. I wake up feeling good. Maybe it's happening because of Brother Tom's herb tea. All the Brothers drink it. One day I went to the monastery to sign something and my signature came out in a scribble. My hand shook and rambled across the bottom half of the page. I had to hold my writing hand steady with my other hand to get the job done. I get hand tremors at unexpected times.

Brother Tom watched me sign the papers. He didn't interfere or offer to help. After the papers were signed, giving him the right to drive, sell, or donate the royal blue 1952 two door convertible Nash Rambler Airflite Convertible Landau, with the original engine and three speed manual transmission, clutch starter, by the book hood ornament, whitewalls, demure artistic oval taillights, original factory chrome with practically no pitting, and fender skirts I had refurbished, we strolled outside.

"Okay," Brother Tom said, looking up at the sky. He hesitated. "I got a secret to tell you. I hope I don't offend you."

Then he told me about the tea. Now there are other teas out there that claim to help you be calm and such, but this stuff goes way beyond that. For the first time, the stillness in me isn't empty. It spends its time touching the hem of ancient wisdoms hidden in the berries that travel clear from China to make tea to fortify old hermits like us. Yeah, I got them on the tea, too.

The emptiness is slowly and steadily filling with a smooth, knowing calmness. A kind of peace. A modest tempo dawning in the stillness. Steadiness beginning to take place within during the tempests. That's what Miss Emma calls the times when we lose our Equanimity.

I was never able to stop losing my Equanimity when I got stirred up. I just handled it so it didn't show. I either vacated the premises whenever possible or tried to stay still and unnoticed as possible. I remembered something I heard long ago describing people.

"Is it okay if we dress up as you for Halloween?" the girl asked. The Monster answered, "It is only fair, because the rest of the year we dress up as you."

It was best to stay here in the monastery on the edge of a national park where it snowed like the devil all winter long. That kind of geography doesn't appeal to most people, and that's the best news we could have.

We also drink that new ale the brothers have been experimenting with lately. It goes real well with the tea. We have gates to keep the unwanted others out and we have each other for companionship. Miss Emma was right. This is the place for us. The three of us have lived our lives in shades of black and white. Some of the gray shades of our lives are almost silver now and softer than before. We do not want any colors or any loud laughs, or fat hugs or clingy touches. We never did.

Map Girl calls us the Three Magi. She seems to think the map I gave her was a special gift. I don't know why. But Miss Emma and William the Dude are coming here a few days before Christmas, so we can caravan back to the store where our precious Map Girl lives. They tell us there will be other misfits there that we will like. We will see. It will be the first Christmas away from Ardenville for us. Whenever I think of it, I have to drink more of Tom's homemade tea and find a carburetor to tune up. Right now I am working on a 1953 Ford.

Each day melts easy into the next for us in this hidden, out of the way place. If and when us three rusty old introverts need to travel any further to escape from others, or to examine more of life from a distance, we have our finely tuned land yachts ready to go. My classic 1930 black Chevy Coupe, Ben's classy 1951 pale blue and white Dodge Coronet Coupe, and Andy's Rambler, a 1952 wood paneled station wagon tuned up and ready to go, all of them just waiting for another road trip.

The Desert Store Series

Susan Sugar Diamond

Away in a Manger

Book # 4

Mama loses Cowboy Johnson in the summer and flees to Emma's ranch to hide out with his ashes just before Christmas. A huge blizzard stops most of the usual misfits from traveling home to the desert store for the annual Christmas gathering. But the desert store doesn't stay empty. Arrivals are expected. Timmon, Hector, and Annie await the appearance of Cowboy Johnson's angry father Matthew but unexpected guests show up first, beginning with Susan Sugar Diamond and Lana English. Perry, Matthews other son, is out the ranch with William the Dude, Emma, and Mama. An intensely moving and luminous accidental gathering of people who have reached a crossroads in their lives.

9 781736 946046